A
Code
of the Heart

JACKI DELECKI

First Print Edition
ISBN 978-0-9863264-0-0

Published by Doe Bay Publishing, Seattle, Washington.
Cover Design by The Killion Group, Inc.
Interior Formatting by Author E.M.S.

Published in the United States of America.

To H.P. with all my love.

ACKNOWLEDGMENTS

Thank you to my extraordinary team. Karuna, my remarkable plot partner, Valerie Susan Hayward, my amazing editor, and to Nancy Mayer, Regency researcher extraordinaire. Any errors in historical facts are my own mistakes or my imagination running amok.

And much gratitude to my support team who keep me writing. Maria Connor, Jen Rice, and my wondrous children.

PROLOGUE

Miss Amelia Bonnington braced herself as the crowd bumped and pushed, straining to get close to His Highness. The crème of society shoved and elbowed, politely-of-course, since one would never want to be accused of bad manners.

The Prince of Wales stood on a small platform elaborately decorated with heavy boughs of greenery and red velvet, matching the Christmas décor of the massive ballroom. Hundreds of beeswax candles burned. No expense had been spared for the house party celebrating his royal visit.

Amelia had no desire to be part of the prince's circle; they were a ghastly group interested only in themselves and their own pleasure.

She sucked in the little air left in the room and pushed, courteously-of-course, toward the door. The crowd and the heat were unbearable. She wasn't one to swoon, but with the thick mix of perfume and the hot bodies, she felt tonight might be her first. She, one of the steadiest women, felt unsteady and unsafe. The last days of upheaval must have had a greater effect on her than she wanted to believe.

Her whole world had been turned upside down and twisted sideways at this house party. In the last two days, her friends had been poisoned and held captive, and she had been ensnared in the French villain's trap. But the deadly crisis had to be kept secret. Nothing must look out of the ordinary. No one outside the intelligence world must ever know about the enemy's threat to the Prince of Wales's life. The ball must go on.

Amelia looked over her shoulder for the closest exit, but the throng pushed her forward. She needed to escape from the packed room.

A gentleman used the chaos in the crowded room to crash into her, to take liberties with her person. After spending the last four years in congested ballrooms, she fully recognized the scoundrel's ploy. His heavy eyelids didn't conceal his hungry eyes as he focused down her cleavage. As he remained fixated on her breasts, he grabbed her elbow, pretending to help her when in fact he intended to pull her close against his hefty, malodorous body.

His reek of stale alcohol and sour sweat constricted her stomach and burned her throat. She pulled her arm away from his grasp, repulsed by the wetness seeping through his gloves. "Sir, release me this instant." She was about to dig her heel into the supposed gentleman's fat toe when suddenly a space opened around her and a smell of fresh lime soap surrounded her.

The perspiring man stared behind her. His slack mouth and his blood-shot eyes widened in fear.

She recognized Lord Brinsley's scent without needing to turn; he was an impossibly difficult, yet irresistibly appealing man. His deep, velvety voice flitted down her skin like a caress. "Miss Amelia, may I escort you away from this mob?"

Relief, and something much more potent, buzzed all her nerve endings. She turned quickly and found herself pressed against the broad chest of the man she had been forced to conspire with to help her friends.

She hastily straightened herself. "I never thought I'd be happy to see you." She refused to be like all the other women who fawned for his slightest glance.

He lifted an eyebrow and the corner of his mouth in that

sardonic way she always found irritating. He was too big, too handsome, and too confident for her to find him irresistible. She'd never let him have the satisfaction of knowing she found him…almost irresistible.

She had loved her childhood hero, since she was eleven years old, but her response to this virile man left her unsteady, unsure of who she was, or what she believed. She was suddenly overwhelmed with the desire to wrestle him to the ground, crawl on top of him, and pummel him. What she would do to him afterwards, she didn't know. And she didn't want to explore why the thought left her breathless and agitated.

Perhaps the whole spy business left her shaky and out of sorts. She needed to get back to London, back to her safe world of fashion and routines. She'd had enough of assassination plots and French spies.

He took her by the elbow and turned her toward the exit. "What is going on in that convoluted mind of yours? I hope the object of your fury was that slimy worm and not me." His full mouth grew into a genuine grin.

How did he read her so easily?

His smile made her feel light-headed and giddy like a silly schoolgirl. Giddiness was not something she had ever experienced until meeting him. With four brothers, she was used to handling men and their superior attitudes. She pulled out of his grasp, but was shoved by an ostentatious matron.

"As wonderful as it is to feel you against me, do you want my escort or not?" His voice rumbled deep in his chest.

She let out a gush of hot air that had been building in her lungs. "You, sir, are no gentleman."

There was a quick flash of hurt in his eyes before he raised his eyebrow in the maddening way. "I know, and that's why all the ladies like me." He emphasized the word "ladies."

The fear and frustration of the last harrowing days gathered in her chest and throat, making it hard to draw air.

"You look as if you're about to combust. Let's go, Red." Her hand disappeared into his enormous fist and he led her through the crowd. His giant size quickly opened a clear path toward the hallway and the closest exit.

His hand was surprisingly comforting for someone so overbearing. Grateful to finally escape the din and the heat with the promise of fresh air and space, she could almost forgive him for his insulting nickname. He had started calling her "Red" in private to bug her, and it had infuriated her just like he knew it would. Like her four brothers had done her entire life, all because of her fiery red hair and her pale white skin that blushed horridly with the slightest provocation.

Once out of the crowded ballroom, he turned and asked her, "Would you like to walk to the conservatory? I'm sure it won't be teeming with the hordes."

"Yes, please."

He took her elbow and led her down a small hallway, away from the noise.

"I needed to get away from the prince's admirers."

"Degeneracy, lechery, and adultery not your favorite pastimes?" He chuckled. "Fashion, right?"

How did he do it? With those two simple words, he'd made her passion for art and design sound trivial.

Anger and resentment from the years of her brothers' teasing and from the last stressful days swirled into a fermenting mass in her chest. It was all made worse by a sick feeling that he might be correct. She took a slow, deep breath, but she couldn't hide the hitch in her breathing even though she tried; her safe world would never be the same.

With the threat of French invasion, her love of art wouldn't help in defending her country. She searched for her usual outrage and anger, but all she felt was a muddle of helplessness and loss.

Nothing made sense anymore.

He pulled on her arm and turned her toward him. "What is it? What's wrong?" His usual taunting tone was gone, replaced by concern and compassion.

She shook her head. "You're right. With the impending war,

fashion is frivolous." She remembered how excited she'd always been with the newest designs, the newest innovations in dress construction. "I'm…" She couldn't swallow against the lump swelling in her throat and the tears burning behind her eyes.

He smoothed her cheek with the back of his knuckles.

"Tears from my favorite red-haired hoyden?" Although his words were teasing, his touch was gentle, caressing. "There is nothing frivolous about you."

She gulped against the sweet words and the way she wanted to throw herself into his arms, to feel his comfort. She rubbed at her eyes, anticipating how blotchy her fair skin would become when she cried.

"What is wrong, Amelia? Did someone hurt you or insult you in the ballroom? Tell me and I'll make sure he never hurts you again."

She looked up into his green eyes, the color of spring with flecks of burnished yellow. "No one insulted me. I'm fine."

"You're not fine. Usually you want to take my head off. Talk to me—I don't recognize you when you're all emotional like this."

She could only shake her head. Like her brothers, he was trying to tease her out of her sudden wretchedness. Fear for her brothers with the impending war made the security of her home and family seem even farther away.

"You've been through a lot in the last few days with Ash's poisoning and then Gwyneth's kidnapping. It's not surprising if it's finally catching up with you. It happens to me too, after I've been on a mission."

"It does?" She looked up at his chiseled face and his springtime eyes. All she could think of was taking shelter in his arms, and then the vision evolved and he was kissing her.

Living in the daydream, she leaned closer to him, offering her lips. She wanted… She didn't know what she wanted except Lord Brinsley's kiss at this moment.

Touching her lightly with his fingertips, he smoothed her cheek, her lips, and down her throat. He paused where her pulse leapt and bounded under his seductive touch.

He put his mouth on hers.

She froze, suspended in the sensation of his soft, warm lips. The rest of the world, the war, the ball, vanished.

With his tongue, he gently traced the seam of her lips. The touch threatened to make her knees melt, and drive the air from her lungs. She parted her lips. With a shaky breath came his tongue, exploring the inside of her mouth.

A moan escaped her. She pressed against him, wanting to be closer, to feel the heat and the security of his arms.

His large hands pulled her tight, burning like coals against her bare back. He ravaged her lips, her throat, her exposed shoulders. "Say my name. I want to hear Derrick on your lips."

"Oh, Derrick."

He deepened the kiss, thrusting his tongue into her mouth, setting off fireworks in her brain. His hard breathing and his powerful body excited her. His usual superior calm was gone. He was a hungry man ready to consume her. He groaned and his hands went down her back to her buttocks. He caressed and explored, lifting her against his erection, causing tremors to shoot through her body.

"I hear voices coming this way," he growled, his voice low and husky.

"What?" Lights flickered in the hallway, but she was unaware of anything else but Derrick.

CHAPTER ONE

London
January, 1803

Brinsley stood in front of the blazing fire in Lord Rathbourne's library. He wasn't cold, but he didn't feel comfortable sitting down while he waited. His hands were sweating, and his heart thundered in his chest. He and Lord Rathbourne had already resolved any bad feeling caused by his blunder of allowing Rathbourne's brother-in-law to be shot on his watch.

How in the hell could a man be so unlucky that his superior would marry the sister of the man he was guarding in Paris? All things considered, his first meeting with Lord Rathbourne had gone better than expected. But today's sudden summons filled Brinsley with a sense of approaching alarm.

He turned to the sound of the door opening. Not Rathbourne, but Ashworth. His dread switched channels so fast it made him dizzy. This meeting was not about national security or French spies; it was going to be about an erotic interlude with Ashworth's fiancée's close friend. That he couldn't stop thinking of the searing, passionate response of Amelia Bonnington at the Edworth ball, wasn't going to be the point of today's confrontation.

"Ashworth." Best to take the initiative with men like Ashworth. "I thought I was to meet with Lord Rathbourne."

"You will be, after I'm finished with you." Ashworth's chin was thrust forward and his shoulders squared.

Brinsley's scowl deepened and his muscles tightened at Ashworth's rigid stance and threatening choice of words.

Ashworth walked to the small table situated between the chairs in front of the fireplace. He poured himself a snifter of brandy. It was never a good sign when Ashworth didn't offer libations.

"Be seated." Ash pointed to one of the chairs.

Ashworth had earned a reputation as a fearless undercover agent. He didn't look the least intimidated in the slightest by Brinsley's larger size. He surpassed Ashworth by at least a head and outweighed him by five stone.

Brinsley strode to the chair and sat. His hands gripped the armrests. He had no choice but to wait. He surmised Ashworth's dark looks and barely-controlled hostility were about a certain red-haired vixen.

Ashworth did not sit; instead he paced like a panther on the prowl, turning on him from a point before the fireplace. His eyes narrowed on Brinsley's face. "You owe this civilized meeting to Lady Gwyneth. If it weren't for her..." His voice was a coarse growl.

Brinsley clenched and unclenched his hands on the armrests. He'd like to see Ashworth try. Unlike Ashworth, he'd been in enough brawls to be unfazed by the possibility of a gentlemanly fight.

"Miss Amelia has made it clear to Lady Gwyneth that you didn't coerce her, and it was only the extreme emotions brought on by the incredible circumstances of the situation that made her weak to your advances."

Advances? It took all of Brinsley's control to disallow Ashworth that it was the lady who initiated the embrace. But as a gentleman, he couldn't mention the fact that Amelia Bonnington had pressed herself against him, seeking to be embraced, wanting to be kissed.

Ashworth stepped closer to lean over him. "My God, man. She's an innocent."

Brinsley tried to control his response; when he remembered the way Amelia's tongue had dueled with his in the passionate kiss. It was proof she was not so innocent—not after that kiss.

"And with your reputation." Ashworth's jaw tightened. "What the hell?"

Brinsley bristled with the reminder that he still wasn't fit to be allowed in English society. "It was a very difficult time for everyone."

"Yes, the strain was incredible for all of us when Lady Gwyneth disappeared, taken by the French in retaliation. But both ladies conducted themselves with incredible bravery and fortitude."

Ashworth was pitiful the way his voice got wistful with the mention of his fiancée. He never understood what made brave men act like fools once they fell into a woman's web.

Ashworth cleared his throat. "The salient fact is, that the lady has refused to have any connection with you. She made it quite clear to Lady Gwyneth that her interests lie elsewhere."

Brinsley stiffened in his chair, ready to spring. Of all the nerve. Amelia Bonnington had been willing to explore her virginal passion with him, but he wasn't good for anything beyond that.

He leaned back in the chair and crossed his legs, acting bored with this newest information. "Who is the man she *is* interested in?"

He didn't bother to mention that the only reason she was still a virgin was because of his sense of honor and control. And she had the nerve to reject him, like this no less.

"I can't divulge the lady's secrets. Lady Gwyneth would have my hide." Ash threw back the last of his brandy and laughed. He didn't seem to mind mentioning Lady Gwyneth's control over him.

Ashworth stepped close, looming over him. "Listen, man. I owe you a debt of gratitude for helping Lady Gwyneth when I was in bad shape. Miss Amelia grew up with Cord's wife, Lady Henrietta, and if Cord ever discovered your dalliance, he'd have you shipped back to France. That is if you remained alive after

Miss Amelia's brothers—all giants I might add—tore you apart for trifling with their sister."

Brinsley thrust himself to his feet, forcing Ash to take a step back. He didn't need Ashworth to be warning him off. He'd make a point of giving Miss Amelia Bonnington a wide berth from now on. What did he want with a seductive, red-haired siren? There were many women who didn't hold his reputation against him.

"It seems the lady has escaped a disastrous connection." He tried to sound flippant, but knew he had failed by Ashworth's spy-honed appraisal. He couldn't help that he had carnal dreams of the sensual Amelia Bonnington in his bed.

With the sound of the door opening, they both turned to find Lord Rathbourne, the formidable spy and their intimidating superior, saunter into the room. "Gentlemen."

Relaxed and smiling, he slapped his friend on the back. "Ash, I'm glad you could join us. Gwyneth will be thrilled to see you. She's in the morning room with Miss Amelia."

Brinsley was disgusted with himself that his stomach curled with longing at the mention of a woman who had made it clear she wanted no part of him.

"They're examining fabrics. I know how much you enjoy discussing fashion with the ladies." Lord Rathbourne bent over the table and poured a glass full of ruby red liquid. He looked up at Brinsley. "Would you care for a drink?"

"Thank you." Brinsley nodded.

Ash offered his glass for Lord Rathbourne to top off his brandy. "I'm happy to discuss anything that makes Gwyneth happy. How is Lady Henrietta feeling today?"

Rathbourne chuckled. "I'm unable to convince her to rest. She is used to taking care of everyone. I had to employ my skills of persuasion to get her to take it easy today. When needed, I can be very convincing."

Brinsley couldn't believe his ears. The Head of British Intelligence was admitting that he had difficulty negotiating with his wife.

Rathbourne ran his fingers through his black hair and looked at Brinsley. "We're very excited by the birth of our first child, but the doctor was very clear that my wife needs to rest each day."

Brinsley didn't know what to say or where to look as his superior discussed his wife's condition. He nodded his head.

Rathbourne took a big mouthful of the brandy. "Excuse me. You'll understand when it's your wife." He raked his hair back again. "Let's get down to business." He walked to his desk and opened a file.

"I received information late last night that there was a man with a great deal of funds in *Ship's Aground* tavern. Surveillance says he's been asking a lot of questions about the Navy's secret weapon."

Ashworth sat down on a chair in front of the desk. "We aren't going to be able to dismiss this information if we don't know anything about the secret weapon."

Lord Rathbourne gestured to Brinsley to take the empty chair. "I've been cleared to give you the information."

"A little late, don't you think?" Ash turned to Brinsley. "It's a bit ironic. The Navy wants our protection, but doesn't trust us enough to tell us what we're protecting."

"They're quite adamant about keeping their plans under French radar. Now that they realize the threat is credible, they are much more forthcoming," Rathbourne added.

"Great. Do tell." Ash leaned back in his chair.

"The Navy has been working with an American inventor, Robert Fulton. Do you remember Ash, when we discovered he was working for the French on an underwater boat? He changed allegiances last year."

Ash laughed. "To the highest bidder?"

"There is a story there for another occasion," Rathbourne said.

"You're telling us our secret weapon is an underwater boat?" Ash was incredulous.

"No, that invention failed miserably, but it has evolved. He kept the closed design device, weighted it with lead so it will ride low in the water, and stabilized it with wooden pontoons. It will be filled with explosives. A man maneuvers it with a paddle."

Ash scoffed. "So the man steers a floating bomb with a paddle! And we thought our work was dangerous."

"The operator is camouflaged, wearing dark clothes and a black cap."

"That makes it sound even riskier." Ash laughed.

"These are difficult times with difficult jobs for everyone. We have our job; protect the secret of this newest weapon." Lord Rathbourne's lack of humor was stark by comparison.

The playful mood dampened with the reminder of the very real and very close threat of French invasion.

"We are sure the French know of our secret weapon?" Ash asked.

"We have to assume the worst and work from there. We've been spreading misinformation about the project."

"Misdirection?" Ash sat forward in his chair.

"Exactly. With the number of men working on the project, it's near impossible to hide that we're building a special boat."

"Did the Navy devise any safe guards for the boat's secrecy?" Brinsley asked.

"The work was subdivided in the earlier stage so no group knew the final project, but now, with final assembly and an impending launch date, the need for our involvement is vital."

"Back to the man paddling a bomb in the dark, deep Channel water. Does he jump in the water and try to swim away?" Ash asked.

"He first must attach the boat to a French ship with a grappling hook. The launch has a timing device to detonate the explosives so he has the time to make a speedy exit. Of course, that is all assuming the French don't see him and blow him out of the water."

Ash exhaled slowly through pursed lips. "Amazing. But tricky for them to get close enough to attach the 'secret weapon' to the ship, right?"

"Exactly, but the Navy assures me that it can be used decisively against the ships Napoleon is amassing in Boulogne. Our job is to keep the knowledge of the weapon and the timing mechanism out of French hands. Nothing about the ship building should alert suspicion, but we can't be sure if the French are after the design of the weapon, the timing mechanism, its current location and impending launch date, its planned target, or how many are being built."

"Do we know what the man tried to buy?" Brinsley asked.

"My source said he offered jewels for any projects Robert Fulton was working on."

"Interesting. But he might just be on a fishing expedition," Ash said.

"That's the most likely conclusion. The French might be throwing around a lot of money to see what they can get. But the more disturbing possibility is that they've discovered the secret weapon and are trying to buy the plans."

"Does the Navy suspect any breach of security?" Ash asked.

"No, they reassured me that Fulton and his assistants haven't been compromised."

"Our job is to find the man trying to buy secrets?" Brinsley asked.

"Exactly. I want you to find the buyer and negotiate to sell the secrets, Brinsley. With your body size, you look like you could work on the docks. And from what I know about you, you know how to handle yourself in the seedy taverns."

Brinsley's spine stiffened. He didn't like the idea that Lord Rathbourne knew about his disreputable past, but of course he did. He was Head of Intelligence.

"What description do you have of this man?" Brinsley asked.

"He spoke like a gentleman, but had his hat pulled down so his face couldn't be totally seen in the shadows."

"Why is he negotiating with jewels?" Brinsley continued.

"It is easier to smuggle jewels out of France than silver. That he's using jewels makes me believe this is not a government-sanctioned plan, but rather an independent smuggling ring," Rathbourne said.

"I don't follow why you don't think Napoleon's behind the plot," Brinsley said.

"Napoleon wouldn't bother with jewels, he'd send silver directly to his agents. Jewels have a way of disappearing."

Rathbourne looked squarely at Brinsley. "Ash has spent some time on the docks and bars in the East End. He's checked out the tavern."

"*Ship's Aground* is the place for our traitor to sell secrets. It's the center of underground business transactions," Ash said.

"Ash can make the connections for you to start your surveillance. Of course, totally incognito," Rathbourne added.

The door flew open. Lady Gwyneth strode into the room with Miss Amelia Bonnington following. Of all his luck, Brinsley was forced to see Amelia when he was starting to settle into his new, risky assignment. The men rose with the ladies' entrance.

"Brompton just told me that my wayward fiancé was in the house and didn't come to greet me," Lady Gwyneth said.

Ash took Lady Gwyneth's hands between his, bringing them up to kiss her knuckles. "Darling, I was coming to you as soon as we finished."

Amelia hung back from the couple. Brinsley's skin prickled with a sudden hypersensitive awareness of Amelia's proximity. Her honeysuckle scent filled his senses, threatening to blank out all else in the room. She had a gardenia pinned to a hairband that held her flowing copper hair away from her face. The white petals of the flower were like her skin: translucent, delicate...beautiful.

They stared at each other, unable to look away. Amelia's porcelain skin colored and a flush rose on her chest and up her neck. He remembered how soft her skin had felt and how he had sucked on the hot, soft flesh.

Ash, as if understanding Amelia's discomfort, wrapped his arm around her, planting a kiss on her cheek in a brotherly fashion. "Amelia, how are the designs coming?"

Possessiveness surged through Brinsley. His body tightened with Ash touching Amelia. What the hell was wrong with him? He hadn't really come to grips with the fact that Amelia wasn't his.

The way her eyes had darkened and her lips parted when she saw him, convinced him that she remembered their kiss. If that's what you could call their kiss—the incredible, blustering heat that exploded between them in the darkened hallway was far more than just a kiss.

"I hope we're not interrupting anything important, Cord," Lady Gwyneth said coyly. "What are you gentlemen working on? French spies conspiring to kill Ash?"

"Gwyneth," Ash scolded.

She hid a lady-like snort behind her fingers.

"Completely boring stuff. Nothing as exciting as Elwood's house party." Rathbourne winked at his sister. "We'll return to business once you've confirmed that your affianced is in no danger."

"You promised that Ash would have no more dangerous assignments before the wedding." Lady Gwyneth looked at her fiancé. Her face shone warm with obvious adoration.

Emptiness filled Brinsley. Witnessing the love shining in Lady Gwyneth's face, he suddenly felt envious of Ash.

Lady Gwyneth released Ash's hands and offered her outstretched hand to him. "Brinsley, this is a pleasant surprise to find you here."

Brinsley bowed over her hand. "It is a pleasure to see you, my lady. And looking so well."

"Cord, I don't believe I've shared with you how incredibly helpful Brinsley was in assisting me when Ash was ill. Without his cool, steady manner, I'm not sure what we would've done. Isn't that so, Amelia?"

Amelia's violet eyes widened as she bit down on her full pink lip. "Yes, he was most helpful." She avoided looking at him, keeping her eyes on Rathbourne.

Brinsley couldn't stop staring at her lips. "Your sister and

Miss Amelia would've handled anything that needed to be done without me, but I'm glad that I could be of assistance."

Not allowing him to escape, Lady Gwyneth clung to Brinsley's hand. "You must join us for tea, Lord Brinsley. Amelia and I are working on my wedding dress, but when you men are finished with this important meeting, please come to the morning room. Uncle Charles and Edward have gone off to their reading club, *The Odd Set of Volumes,* so it will be only us. Henrietta will be up from her nap by then."

Brinsley bowed over Lady Gwyneth's hand, his mind racing for a plausible reason to decline. "Thank you, my lady, but…"

Lady Gwyneth placed her hand on his arm. "I won't take 'no' for an answer. After our experience together I feel as if we are well acquainted; you simply must join us."

Ash pulled Lady Gwyneth close to him and whispered in her ear, loud enough for Brinsley to hear him say, "You don't need to keep touching him."

Lady Gwyneth stared into Ash's eyes. Her look of longing was painful for a lonely man to watch.

Rathbourne cleared his throat.

Lady Gwyneth laughed merrily.

Ash turned to Brinsley. "We will understand if you have other commitments."

Brinsley had planned to decline, but was now determined to accept after Ashworth's attempt to cut him away. "I couldn't disappoint the ladies."

The look Ash gave him was very clear. He was not to get any ideas about Miss Amelia Bonnington.

CHAPTER TWO

Amelia's heart beat a vicious tattoo against her chest. The incessant hammering had persisted since she had first learned that Lord Brinsley was at the Rathbourne house.

After her inexplicable, impulsive, uncharacteristic behavior, she'd hoped to never cross paths with the rogue again. She had completely blocked out his work as an agent. Besides being a rake, the man was a spy.

The conversation around afternoon tea had remained polite, although Amelia couldn't ignore the prickly awareness of the gargantuan man who dwarfed the chair across from her. He leaned back, insolently crossing a broad leg over the other.

"Amelia has outdone herself with the design of my wedding ball gown," Gwyneth gushed to Ash.

Ash whispered to Gwyneth, "You look beautiful in anything."

The intimacy in his look and the way his voice deepened made Amelia look away from the couple.

Gwyneth caught her lower lip between her teeth in a delicate nip that was unable to hide her mischievous smile. The charged tension between the couple shot like a bolt of lightning through the sunny morning room.

Henrietta, still pale after her nap, with dark circles under eyes, sipped her tea, ignoring the heated looks and sparks between the couple. "With Gwyneth's tall stature and deportment, creating her wedding gown must have made it much easier than designing mine."

Gwyneth turned in her chair. "But Henrietta, you looked like a tiny fairy princess on your wedding day. I'll never forget the look on my brother's face. I would never have thought that either of these gentlemen, what with their rakish reputations, would finally fall in love."

Henrietta laughed. "I'm afraid I'm no fairy princess. But you are correct about Cord. He did have quite a reputation."

"Cord should be here to defend himself." Ash coughed behind his hand. "You know much of his reputation was attributable to his work."

Gwyneth rolled her eyes and turned to Ash. "Was your reputation part of your cover too?"

"Gwyneth…" Ash pleaded. Seeking to change the subject, he turned to Amelia. "Please tell us how you go about designing a gown?"

Gwyneth snorted then coughed into her tea. Between sputters, she teased Ash. "James Henry Ashworth, you know you have no interest in the stitch and tuck of dress making. You're just trying to change the subject from your devilish past."

Ash shook his head. "I was simply engaging in polite discourse with Miss Amelia."

Henrietta passed the tray that had been filled with finger sandwiches, cookies, biscuits, cheese, and slices of apple. Mrs. Brompton had sent a hearty repast knowing the gentlemen would be present.

With four brothers, Amelia was very aware of men's hearty appetites. The thought of Lord Brinsley's voracious appetite was speeding up her heart again. He and Ash had almost cleared the entire tray of food except for a few lonely biscuits and cheese.

"Brinsley, please, you must finish the rest of the biscuits. Mrs. Brompton will take it as a personal affront if any food remains."

"Thank you. You have an amazing cook." His broad hand moved the two biscuits and cheese to his plate in one graceful move.

Amelia's chest tightened with the memory of how he had rubbed her lower lip with that massive hand before he kissed her. She took a slow breath and pressed her hand against her chest, trying to ease the constriction on her lungs and speeding heart.

"Brinsley, I'm sure wedding gowns are of no interest to you. Ash has to pretend since he's an affianced man. Do you have any sisters?" Gwyneth asked.

Amelia wasn't sure if Gwyneth remembered the scandal surrounding Lord Brinsley—that he didn't appear in good ton because of his reputation. Gwyneth probably did remember, but disregarded the rumors about him running off with his brother's fiancée, or she simply didn't care now that she'd included him in her inner circle of friends.

Amelia wasn't as forgiving. She had no trouble believing the seduction rumors after the way he had kissed her. A familiar heat stole up from her stomach, to her chest, to her face. She hated that her pale skin reflected all her emotions. Right now, the cad was watching her over the rim of his teacup and appeared to know that the memory of their inflamed embrace had caused her skin to turn the color of a pomegranate.

Henrietta also watched, knowing that something was afoot.

Amelia had wanted to spare her closest friend from her turbulent feelings surrounding the Christmas house party, knowing that Henrietta was suffering badly from morning sickness.

"I've no sisters. Only an older brother." Lord Brinsley showed no difficulty speaking about his family and no discomfiture specifically speaking about his brother.

"Well, we'll have to make up for your lack of sisters, won't we, Henrietta, Amelia?" Gwyneth asked innocently.

Sisters? What game was Gwyneth playing? Was she trying to be a matchmaker? Gwyneth blissfully ignored the harsh look Amelia hurled at her friend.

Gwyneth had wanted all the details of their romance after witnessing their embrace—as if one embrace counted for a romance, even one long, lingering, unforgettable moment.

Damn it. With Gwyneth's intense, questioning look, the heat came in waves again. The idea that both Gwyneth and Ash had observed the intense dalliance appalled her. She'd never ask how much they'd seen—not that Gwyneth wouldn't be thrilled to discuss every delicious scintillating moment in glorious detail.

Henrietta leaned forward in her chair. "I'd be pleased to have another brother, Lord Brinsley. Gwyneth has told me all about your heroic role at Christmas time. I don't know what Cord would've done if anything had happened to Ash."

"Henrietta, you're embarrassing Ash. Men never admit to their feelings about each other," Gwyneth teased. "Can you imagine Cord declaring his love for Ash?"

Henrietta laughed out loud, as did Gwyneth.

Usually Amelia would've joined in, but she sat stiff, unable to banter while Brinsley watched her every move, noting her every reaction. Even when he wasn't looking at her, she knew he was as aware of her as she was of him.

"I'd be pleased to call each of you charming ladies sisters." Now Lord Brinsley's green eyes deepened to a mysterious gray as he gave Amelia a challenging look. He was fully aware that he didn't arouse sister-like feelings in her.

Gwyneth clapped her hands in delight. "How wonderful since I only have Cord." A wistful look darkened Gwyneth's face. Although young and impetuous, Gwyneth was sensitive and had suffered in her childhood with the loss of her oldest brother.

"You only have Cord? What about me?" Ash stood up and lifted Gwyneth from the settee into his arms. "Excuse us, I've got to explain to Lady Gwyneth a few things about who she has in her life."

Laughing and pretending to fight to be released, Gwyneth batted at Ash's chest. "Put me down, you brute." All efforts at her command were negated by her laugh.

Halfway to the door Ash turned and addressed Henrietta. "Aunt Euphemia isn't home, is she?"

Henrietta, the most serious of the trio, giggled at the question.

"You don't have to worry. Aunt Euphemia is on her social calls."

Gwyneth leaned back in Ash's arms and looked up at him with a highly amused twinkle in her eyes. "You're not afraid of criminals and spies, but you're wary of dear Aunt Euphemia."

"You shouldn't insult me when you're in such a vulnerable position." Ash pretended to drop Gwyneth who squealed in response. "And any intelligent man would be afraid of your Aunt Euphemia."

"Brinsley, my man, can you get the door? As you can see I have my hands full."

The loving way Ash spoke caused a slight ache to start in Amelia's chest. Both of her closest friends had found love. They both were radiant with joy. She felt left out of the warmth.

Henrietta watched the couple leave, then stood. "I think I'll check on my wayward husband. Amelia, can you entertain Lord Brinsley for a few minutes while I make sure that Cord has had tea? Once he starts working, he forgets to eat."

Her closest friends abandoned her to a man with a questionable reputation. Were they insane, or was she? She should have followed Cord's example and found a way to stay away. Her stomach and heart fluttered in anticipation as she watched Lord Brinsley walk toward her. His black riding breeches hugged his powerful thighs. There was something very threatening in his slow meander as if he was preparing to pounce.

Why did she suddenly feel threatened? His male posture caused her stomach to flip-flop in a most nerve-racking manner. He was like her brothers—large and dominant, confident in his own power. She remembered being pressed against those thighs, the way he had pushed his leg between hers. A warmth flooded her entire being.

He sat on the settee close to her. As he seated himself beside her, the cushion tipped her closer to him. She resisted the urge to move away; she refused to allow him to believe she was afraid of him. Although her face was crimson, she wasn't about to show any other outward reaction to the rogue's encroaching position. He knew his potent maleness unsettled her. He was used to women fawning over him and his raw virility.

"It seems I owe you an apology." He leaned close, too close. So close she could see flecks of gold in darkened eyes and the beginning of the dusky bristles on his angular jaw.

He spoke of apology, but the way he looked at her was neither repentant nor contrite. In fact, he looked angry. Why should he be angry?

"Lord Brinsley." Her voice came out breathless. She reached for her cup of tea to hide her nervousness. "You do not owe me an apology. I'm not sure why you feel you do."

"It seems Ash witnessed our little embrace and felt it was marriage-worthy."

Amelia gasped. "What?" She froze, her cup forgotten in her surprise. Then fury erupted from deep within. Ash had the nerve to speak to Lord Brinsley? Ash wasn't her brother. This sounded more like Gwyneth's interference. Amelia struggled to breathe. She was mortified and beyond angry. She knew her face burned hotly as did the fire in her gut.

Lord Brinsley watched her carefully, his eyes taking in every inch of her exposed skin.

"Ash spoke to you about me...about marrying me?" She could barely get the words out.

Lord Brinsley's voice was rough and clipped. "He made it obvious that the idea of me as a husband is distasteful to you. You can rest easy; I'm not going to ask. I wouldn't want to embarrass you."

Amelia would've laughed at the absurdity of the situation if she weren't humiliated, furious, and utterly flummoxed by feelings she couldn't identify. "I can't believe Ash took it upon himself... I can't believe he spoke to you about..." She couldn't bring herself to call the episode that had left her sleepless and agitated for weeks a "little embrace." Understanding Ash's concern tempered her anger, but it didn't absolve him. The insolent man next to her was another matter. His casual manner about the passionate interlude had kept her spinning in a daze for days, her emotions ricocheting.

Unable to control the ire, her brothers had labeled her red-haired temper, she blurted out, "I assume you've shared 'little embraces' likes ours all the time and you're still not married."

His jaw tightened and his green eyes turned flinty gray, his voice was a threatening growl. "I've never met a woman who wasn't accommodating. Your problem is you are Lady Gwyneth and Lady Henrietta's friend, and an innocent gentlewoman."

The cad. How dare he refer to his "accommodating women," and he meant more than kissing when he said "accommodating." How ungentlemanly to say that the only reason he felt caught was because of her innocence. "Are you insinuating our embrace wouldn't matter to a man of your experience if I weren't friends with the wives of your associates?"

She took pleasure in watching his strong jaw clench in agitation, the tightening rippled his muscular throat.

"Ash explained to me that I would not be your choice for a husband. And that your desires lie elsewhere."

Anxiety swelled up from her churning stomach, making her light-headed. Ash knew about Michael and had spoken to Lord Brinsley. Was nothing sacrosanct?

"My God, your face is so pale. Are you all right?" Lord Brinsley took her hands in his, rubbing them briskly; they were ice cold.

Of course she was pale—not from shock but from absolute humiliation. She was on the verge of laughing and crying simultaneously. Ash had been protecting her, acting like her brother, but he had bared her childhood infatuation with Michael to a virtual stranger. She felt violated.

Lord Brinsley's hands were warm and his eyes filled with compassion. She wanted to lean into his comfort and strength. With both her friends moving forward with their lives, she felt left behind. But this is exactly how she had ended up in his arms in the first place—her loneliness and her need for comfort.

He leaned toward her as if he might kiss her again when the noise of the door opening alerted them both.

"Amelia, Amelia." Edward, Henrietta's younger brother, ran into the room with Gus, his yellow Labrador. "I'm just back and Brompton told me you were here. Did you remember to bring your breeches?"

Edward looked exactly like his older brother—his curly yellow hair, the blue eyes, and the charming and irresistible Harcourt smile. His resemblance to her childhood infatuation, Michael Harcourt, wrenched something inside Amelia and the memories and youthful fantasies she'd clung to after her world careened out of control with her mother's death, flooded to the surface.

Amelia jumped up from the settee, wrenching her hands free. Lord Brinsley stood as she did, but instead of stepping away, he stepped protectively close.

Edward stared up at Lord Brinsley. "Wow, you're big." And without taking a breath, the next question rushed out of Edward's mouth. "Do you play cricket?"

Amelia couldn't help but chuckle. Lord Brinsley turned and gave her the most irresistible crooked smile. She felt the familiar breathlessness he created in her. It took a minute to look away from this captivating smile on the face of the man who was always scowling.

Remembering herself, she scolded, "Edward, where are your manners?"

"But Amelia, this is perfect weather for us to practice. You promised."

"Edward." Amelia raised her voice, projecting the same commanding tone she used with all her brothers. "This is Lord Brinsley. Lord Brinsley, this ill-mannered young man is Edward, Henrietta's younger brother, and as you can guess, a cricket fiend. And his companion, sitting there all prim and proper, is Gus."

Edward bowed his head toward Lord Brinsley. "It is a pleasure to meet you."

Lord Brinsley bowed deeply to Edward as if meeting a duke. "The pleasure is all mine. And I don't blame you at all for wanting to be outside on such a fine day." He knelt down on one knee and rubbed Gus' head. "Do you fancy cricket as well, old boy?"

"Gus' talent is stealing the ball and making us chase him to get it back." Edward shifted his weight impatiently. "Amelia, can you practice today?"

"Miss Amelia is a cricket player?" Lord Brinsley sounded impressed.

"Amelia is an amazing wicket keeper. If she weren't a girl, she'd be unbeatable."

"Thank you, Master Edward." Amelia curtsied. "Such strong praise indeed."

"But she is a girl." Lord Brinsley's gravelly voice close to her ear sent ripples of sensation down to her toes.

Despite his young age, Edward was very observant, much like his gifted older siblings. He glanced back-and-forth between Lord Brinsley and her. "Does my brother know about him?"

"What?" Amelia's voice came out high, strangled with indignation.

"Michael won't like him paying attention to you, even if Lord Brinsley looks like he could easily pummel him."

"Of all the most ridiculous…"Amelia blustered. She couldn't believe every gentleman, even the young ones, felt compelled to protect her today.

"Edward Michael Harcourt—Silence!" she shouted. Her red-haired temper flared. Drawn by her agitation, Gus came around the table and sat at her feet, placing a giant paw on one of her feet as if trying to calm her.

Edward looked crestfallen, his innocent smile now sheepish. "But…Amelia, you know you're going to marry Michael."

"I know no such thing. And it is not for you to discuss with anyone. It is between Michael and me."

Lord Brinsley had gone utterly immobile. This morning was turning into a nightmare.

"But how will I get to have you as a sister if you don't marry Michael?" Edward's voice was wretched and sincere.

Now she felt like an incredible ogre. Tears burned behind her eyes. She stepped around the table and pulled Edward close to her. "I will always consider myself, first and foremost, your sister, no matter who I marry."

Edward's voice cracked. "Gosh, Amelia. You don't have to go all sappy on me. How will I be able to play cricket if you aren't around?"

Now, Amelia almost burst into a hysterical laugh. She covered her mouth with her hands, but she couldn't prevent the giggles from escaping.

Lord Brinsley chuckled, a low and gruff sound.

Amelia looked up into his laughing eyes. His harsh, angular face had softened, making him look years younger.

Caught in his gaze, she struggled to pull herself together.

"Now that we've aired everything private about me..." Seeing his appreciative look, Amelia didn't feel as embarrassed or exposed as she had earlier.

Edward leaned over the table to pick up the last two biscuits. "Who ate all the food? Gus and I are starved."

"I'm the guilty party," Lord Brinsley said.

"You must eat a lot...with your size." Edward inspected Lord Brinsley carefully. "Are you a bowler?"

"I've played that position."

"Will you play with Amelia and me today? I bet you have a wicked arm."

"Edward, I can't practice today. I'm here to help Gwyneth with her wedding plans."

"How long can wedding plans take? And where is Gwyneth? Is she with Ash again?"

"Yes, she's with Ash. And when she returns, we have to go over details."

Edward also channeled the persistence and doggedness of the Harcourt family. "What about tomorrow? Will you join us, Lord Brinsley? I bet I can get Cord to play. That is, if Henrietta is feeling better. I wish Michael would return home. He's the best bowler. Isn't he, Amelia?"

Where was Michael? Henrietta had told her he was recovering from the bullet wound he sustained in Paris. "How can Michael be on a journey? He's supposed to be at his estate resting from his wound."

Aware of Lord Brinsley's close presence, she heard his sharp intake of breath. Since he already knew that Michael was someone special to her, she didn't have to pretend she wasn't interested.

"I don't know. Henrietta won't tell me. She told me to stop badgering her about him. She said she'd let me know when he returned. Will you play with us tomorrow, Lord Brinsley?"

"I'd be happy to play cricket with you tomorrow, Master Edward—as long as Miss Amelia is willing to join us." The corner of his lip, twisted into a smug smirk.

Edward jumped in place. "Stupendous. Gwyneth will play and I bet if Gwyneth plays we can get Ash to play. It is too bad that Hen can't play, she's an amazing fielder."

Amelia was trapped. She couldn't deny Edward. His enthusiasm was contagious. She tried to give Lord Brinsley what her brother's called her wicked, mean look, but it fizzled upon seeing his roguish grin. She had no choice, but to grin back at him.

"Tomorrow should be an interesting game." His suggestive tone caused her skin to tingle hot and cold. "Will you be wearing breeches?"

Color rose up into her face for the hundredth time today. "No, I will not. But I will plan on my team winning."

And with that challenge, she lifted her chin and marched out of the room in search of Gwyneth.

CHAPTER THREE

Amelia followed Madame De Puis into the large storage room in the back of the modiste's shop to view the newly arrived smuggled treasure.

With England and France at war, the fabulous silks and lace essential for dressmaking couldn't be obtained from France. The contraband bolts of silks, lace, and velvet stretched across the polished wooden worktable.

A singular joy filled Amelia as she took in the rainbow of colors and textures on display. She reverently stroked a supple, pale pink silk with a hue as delicate as the gossamer wings of fairies.

Amelia turned to her friend. "Helene, this feels like Christmas all over again."

Ladies never questioned where the fabrics come from or how they were obtained, but Amelia's frequent visits to the shop and her close relationship with the modiste revealed the full details. Smugglers were the suppliers.

"Yes, Maurice has done well with this shipment." Helene, known to the ton's ladies as Madame de Puis, was the finest modiste in London.

Amelia was surprised by the mention of a name of the smuggler. Helene had always been most discrete.

"The timing of this shipment is perfect for Lady Gwyneth's wedding." Amelia walked around the table. "I want the dress to be in the red palette for the perfect Valentine wedding."

Helene unrolled a bolt of a soft, rose-colored *Peau de Soie*.

"*Un tissu q'elle adore, oui*?" When excited, Helene forgot herself and spoke in French.

Amelia leaned closer to inspect the material called *skin of silk* or *Duchess Satin*. "It's the perfect hue for Lady Gwyneth's wedding ball gown." Amelia was designing yet another gown for another close friend's wedding. She tried not to give in to the melancholy that she wasn't a bride and didn't see becoming one in the near future—she was resigned to designing the wedding dresses, never wearing one.

Helene unrolled the fabric. "The *Peau de Soie* has just the right stiff drape for the design you've drawn, don't you agree?"

Amelia arranged the material over her arm, testing the weight and fold.

"I couldn't be more pleased. Lady Gwyneth will look beautiful in this." Amelia pictured her friend's dramatic black eyes and ebony hair contrasting with the pink-toned dress. Lady Gwyneth was going to make a gorgeous bride.

Amelia's lonely life stretched out in front of her. Soon she'd be designing wedding dresses for Gwyneth's and Henrietta's daughters.

She shook her head. What was wrong with her? She wasn't usually one to dwell on unhappiness. She knew exactly where to lay the blame for her conundrum—Lord Derrick Jeremy Randolph Brinsley's ardent, vehement kiss. Now she understood why her friends always had a silly smile on their faces—passion.

Amelia pulled out the pastel pink chiffon silk that she had first found. "This would be delightful. This chiffon silk is supple and will make a beautiful drape for the veil."

"And what about your dress? We must have you look as beautiful as the bride." Helene's eyes and voice had softened as if she had read the proper reason for Amelia's melancholy.

Amelia attempted a smile. "As only the designer, I can't outshine the bride." But in her heart, she wanted to shock and tantalize a certain gentleman out of his complacency—Michael

Harcourt, the Earl of Kendal, her childhood obsession. She expected him to attend the wedding ball. But why was she having difficulty remembering what he looked like? And why did her mind keep circling around to the ardent embrace with Lord Brinsley and his dazzling smile yesterday at tea?

She had planned to use her dress designs to entice Michael Harcourt in the same manner she had helped Gwyneth capture Ash's attention.

"I want to wear red," Amelia said. She sorted through the pile, looking for the right shade of reddish-purple. As a redhead, she had to be very careful in her selection of reds.

Helene widened her eyes and raised her eyebrows. "*Rouge?*"

"Not deep red." Amelia did fantasize arriving at the ball in a ruby red dress with a revealing décolletage. It obviously worked for Gwyneth, and there wasn't any reason it couldn't work for her. Except Gwyneth had a voluptuous figure and dramatic looks. Unlike her friend, Amelia was tall and thin with very little cleavage. Her mother had called her "willowy," but her brothers, less tactful, called her "beanpole." She did have womanly curves, just not the kind that gentleman found irresistible.

"More the color of raspberries," Amelia added.

"Yes, more on the pink side." Helene concurred.

Amelia hated that she was more of a pastel woman, implying a girlish color versus a bolder red, the color of a passionate woman. Except, with Lord Brinsley. The color in her face began to rise as she remembered her electric response to his demanding hunger.

Helene smiled. "Thinking of someone you'd like to impress, yes? You are a beautiful woman and a stunning artist. Whomever you choose, will be very fortunate to have you as a wife." Helene patted her arm.

Her shared love of all things related to design and fabric had forged a unique friendship with Helene. Ladies were never friends with women who worked in trade, but Amelia had great respect for Helene, both as a designer and a woman who survived terrible things that had occurred in France. Not that Helene ever spoke of her past except to contend that it was "best forgotten." She had made a new life in England.

"Thank you, Helene. I wish I were as confident as you." Her feelings remained confused—she had always dreamed of Michael as her husband, but her thoughts kept returning to Lord Brinsley's hands on her body, and his gruff moans as he pressed against her. She couldn't believe she had allowed the rake to kiss and fondle her as if she were one of his accommodating women. If her brothers ever found out, she'd promptly become bride to a man spurned by society or he'd be found wounded on some dueling field somewhere. The man was not husband material, so why couldn't she forget him?

As Helene turned to speak with one of the shop girls, Amelia explored through the rolls of fabric on a side table. "Helene, you've received fashion dolls in this shipment." Amelia held up two small packages wrapped in silk.

Helen whirled around. "You found them?"

"Yes, they were tucked under this roll of muslin." Amelia rested a hand on the bolt of flower-print cotton.

Helene's manner was clipped and business like. "I received only two dolls. I hope the war will end soon; it is so difficult to stay abreast of French fashion. My ladies care more about fashion than Napoleon conquering the world."

Amelia didn't want to think about the implications of a French invasion for her friend's business. "I'm afraid, with Napoleon's aspirations, the shipments from France will get worse. The Channel is being guarded; French ships are finding reaching England increasingly difficult."

Helene's eyes narrowed. "Amelia, you are a most unusual English lady to have an interest in the war." Then Helene laughed as if she hadn't looked suspiciously at Amelia. "I'm glad for the smugglers who aren't fazed by either French or English warships firing on them."

Amelia didn't mention her source of information being her friend Henrietta.

Helene shook her head. "I think you hope you are right. But, don't worry about me. I didn't believe last year's peace treaty would last, so I bought a full supply of fabrics to stock my shop."

Amelia should've known that her friend would show the French ingenuity in business. "Oh, I'm glad, Helene."

Amelia touched the first of the dolls still wrapped in silk. "Helene, may I see them?"

The French sent dolls, meticulously dressed in the latest fashion, around the world for the ladies to peruse and desire the latest French designs, maintaining the French as the arbitrators and leaders in the world of fashion.

Helene hesitated and then nodded. "Of course. As London's famous fashion authority, you must see them."

Amelia cherished the dolls; they inspired her creativity. The silk lemon-yellow gown on the first doll was of simple lines, but the embroidery of golden vines made the dress resplendent. The porcelain doll's head had a crown of hammered gold vines to match. Wrapped around her arms, was a paisley shawl with amber tones.

Amelia reverently touched the perfect workmanship in miniature. She treasured touching works of beauty. She was adept with the needle, but her greater talent was in drawing. She liked designing—the lines and drapes, the texture and the colors were her passion.

"It is beautiful. And perfect for Lady Henrietta, don't you think?" Henrietta, who cared little about fashion, limited her choice to yellow and green colors and simple lines. She would be happy with this dress.

"Yes, Lady Henrietta does like simple designs, and this lemon-chiffon is perfect for her coloring, but the glimmering vines make it proper attire for a countess. Perfect for her sister-in-law's wedding."

Unwrapping the second doll, Amelia gasped at the sheer beauty and its perfect idea for Gwyneth's wedding ball gown—a cornflower blue dress with an orange tone-red ribbon tied underneath its high-waist. The bodice was fine, like a spider web lace, with the same lace on the hem of the dress with a glorious train trailing behind.

"It is perfect for Lady Gwyneth, yes? The doll's coloring, the dark hair is the same as Lady Gwyneth."

The doll had a red coral necklace, dangling earrings, and bracelets on each arm. The matching crown held the long veil.

Amelia fingered the finely-crafted crown. "It is outstanding."

"The blue is the wrong color for a bride, but the pink-toned fabrics you've chosen will be perfect, and offset the orange tones in the jewelry. With the change in color palette, it will be perfect for Lady Gwyneth."

Amelia was struck breathless at the absolutely exquisiteness of the detail in the doll's clothes and the similarity between her designs. She had wanted Gwyneth to look like a medieval Madonna with her curvaceous body and amiable personality. This veil and gown would create the most dazzling wedding finery.

"Helene, can I borrow these dolls to show Lady Henrietta and Lady Gwyneth?"

The modiste made a handsome sum by charging her customers to see the newest French dolls. "Today? You need to show them so soon?" Helene asked.

Amelia was excited to share the dolls perfection of her vision with her dear friends. "Yes, please, Helene. I can return them tomorrow at the latest if you've promised them to someone else."

Amelia was surprised by Helene's hesitancy. Henrietta and Gwyneth were ladies of significance in the ton, and it seemed strange that Helene wouldn't want to share the dolls with ladies of high standing.

"Yes, of course. I can have Elodie pick them up."

"Whatever you think best, Helene. Or I can bring them back since I want to pick the fabric for Lady Henrietta's gown tomorrow." Amelia felt unsettled by Helene's strange behavior.

All the talk of the English blockade must have been more upsetting to Helene than she let on. Amelia wanted to say something encouraging to her friend, but with war imminent between their two countries, she couldn't pretend to give false assurances.

CHAPTER FOUR

Brinsley sat in a dark corner in the *Ship's Aground* tavern, a damp and murky dockside pub in the East End filled with dockworkers, thugs and every imaginable kind of criminal. The gloomy name matched his mood. One red-haired vixen had run *him* aground. She played cricket in breeches. That image of her rounded derriere in breeches had haunted him since…not that he had actually seen her, but the erotic image that young Edward planted remained emblazoned on his mind.

He shifted on the hard wooden bench, trying to dampen down his rising need. He was back in the spy game, away from innocent women who romped in breeches. His guts were coiled in knots after his day with Amelia. It always boiled down to a woman.

It wasn't only his need for Amelia. He was tired of not belonging anywhere or with anyone. Watching Rathbourne and Ashworth and their ladies, he desperately wanted to belong, to be part of a group of friends who cared about each other, who teased and laughed together. He wished most of all to belong to a certain blushing, gentle-bred woman.

Overflowing with frustration, he felt the urge to knock some heads together and work off a bit of steam. Nothing would give him more satisfaction than to end the day with a brawl.

He avoided looking at Ash, sitting in the opposite corner. He didn't need to look to know that Ash was aware of everything and everyone in the run-down watering hole. They were on a scouting mission, looking for the traitor who was passing Navy secrets or someone willing to pay for those secrets.

They both waited and watched.

A tavern wench approached in a low-cut dress that barely covered her enormous breasts, the material was angled just so to tease a man's thoughts and entice his fingers.

"Why's a big fellow like you sitting all alone?" She leaned over to collect his empty glass, purposefully giving him a good view of her rouged nipples. "Need some company?"

It wouldn't hurt his cover to have a voluptuous lass seated with him. And it helped his male ego to note her sensual appreciation of him reflected in her dark eyes and the "o" of her full mouth. "May I buy you a drink, my lady?"

"You're a funny one." She playfully punched his arm. "My lady—that's a good one."

He gestured toward the space on the bench next to him for her to sit then nodded to the waiter to bring another drink.

"You're new to the pub?" She ran a gritty finger along his arm.

It took a lot not to pull away from her touch and her odor of sweat ill-concealed by her cheap perfume.

"I'm not a regular, but I've been here before."

"I don't think so. I would've remembered someone like you." Her hand had now wandered down his thigh, getting close to the family jewels. "I couldn't possibly forget someone so…big."

He wasn't in the mood to be mauled. Not totally true. He'd love to be mauled, but by a woman with slender, pale fingers and flame red hair.

He grabbed the woman's hand and put it on the table. "You're going to make me embarrass myself."

A waiter, with greasy hair pulled back in a queue, a dirty towel tucked into his breeches, carried over another tankard of ale.

"Hullo, Harry." The dark-haired woman batted her eyelashes at the older man.

"You caught yourself a live one." The waiter winked at him as he put the tankard down.

Brinsley lifted his cup. "To a night at *Ship's Aground* with…?" He glanced at the young woman, eyebrows raised.

"Bev, at your service…anything you'd be needing." She leaned into him, her soft ample curves pressing close.

Brinsley ignored her blatant invitation. "Seems like a quiet night. I heard this place can get rough."

Bev raised her tankard and took a big swig. She wiped the foam from her lips with the back of her sleeve. "When the dock workers get paid…that's when it gets interesting."

"You must be popular. Seems like you know everyone who comes here." He sipped his ale. "You knew I wasn't a regular."

"I knows most of the men." She looked up at him, her eyes narrowed. "You're looking for someone, ain't ya?"

"Why'd you say that?"

"Cuz your likes don't come to places like this."

Shit, had he already blown his cover? Lord Rathbourne would have his ass. And she was only half right. After he had been rejected by his family and friends, he hung out in dives just like this to wash away the taint of good society. "You're right. I'm looking for my hellion brother." In spy lies, always stick as close as you can to the truth. "He has a drinking problem and we haven't seen him in weeks. When he's in a foul mood and in his cups, he goes looking for trouble."

"I could keep an eye open for your brother." Bev lowered her voice, but ran her hand over his arms in a playful manner for anyone watching.

"Could you, now?" He wound a curl close to her face around a finger. He leaned closer. "That would be very helpful."

Her laugh was throaty in an effort to sound sultry. "I got my uses." She then whispered in his ear. "Twenty quid."

By Bev's exorbitant price, she understood the significance of the job. He traced the border of the frayed material along her breasts, giving the impression of a man absorbed. "Done deal."

"Why don't we go upstairs and work out the details." Her hand was back in his crotch. "The tiny, insignificant details."

God, he might not want her, but his partner didn't seem to mind. He laughed out loud as he pried her fingers away. "The waiter was right, you're a live one."

He kept her hand between his. "Tiny, huh?"

She purred. "Not tiny at all."

He pressed his lips to her neck and said low, "My brother is not big like I am. He's short, and likes to pretend he's French."

Bev threw her head back as if enjoying an erotic interlude. "I understand. How will I contact you?"

He continued to keep his head at her neck, but his fingers played in the front of her gown. "I'll contact you."

As he had done many a time paying for a night between the sheets, he reached into his coat and pulled out the coins. He placed the money on the table for all observers to see the transaction.

"I'll be back." He started to stand, searching for Ash who had remained at his table. Now, Ash was in a shoving match with a brawny dockworker who outweighed him by four stone.

Ash threw a punch at the guy and all hell broke loose. Just what Brinsley had needed—a bloody brawl.

Someone grabbed Brinsley by the arm. Swinging around, he was confronted by a giant with a scar across his cheek, broken bottle in his hand, already primed to do damage. He ducked the swinging bottle and landed a punch to the bully's gut. The well-placed punch didn't faze his assailant, only enraging him more.

"You smarmy bastard." The giant swung the jagged bottle as he charged forward.

Brinsley shouted over the din of crashing furniture, breaking bottles, and shouts of aggression. "Come and get me. I'm not afraid of you." Brinsley was immensely entertained by the look on the mammoth's face. At six feet, a full sixteen stone, his assailant was far from little, but the taunt had the desired effect.

Bracing himself, Brinsley kicked as hard as he could, aiming for his opponent's kneecap. When the guy buckled forward, Brinsley positioned his knee and delivered the "piece de resistance" to the guy's groin.

The giant sprawled to the floor, his leg bent wrong and blood streaming from his broken nose and split lip.

Brinsley looked around for Ash, but couldn't locate him in

the chaos. Distracted, he didn't see the guy coming at him from the side until it was too late. Brinsley turned, but the ham-sized fist caught him on the right cheek.

Infuriated by the pain, Brinsley grabbed the man by the neck and twisted. The man fell in a broken heap. It was a wakeup call for Brinsley. This was a brawl—men letting off steam—he understood the difference. But he'd come here already looking for a fight, now the agonizing pain in his face and his worries about Ash was causing him to feel explosive.

He scanned the room for any sign of Ash, but in the dimly lit chaos, it was hard to discern who was on the ground. The door opened and he watched a short man leave and right behind him was Ash. He searched for Bev, but she had also disappeared.

Brinsley made his way through the fighting masses, stepping over a several crumpled bodies. He had to deliver a few more punches before he got to the door. He didn't know what to expect when he got outside, but he hoped to hell he hadn't lost Ash.

CHAPTER FIVE

Amelia reverently unwrapped the doll from its silk coverings. She had packed both dolls in silk scraps from her workshop to protect them on her walk to Rathbourne house. A joyous anticipation raced through her body, as if she were discovering a special Christmas present. She hoped to build the dramatic moment for Gwyneth, anticipating and yearning for the perfect dress for her perfect day.

Amelia watched Gwyneth expectantly. With her ever-expressive face, Gwyneth made it simple to read her emotions and her reaction.

Amelia wanted to accomplish for Gwyneth the same dream she had achieved for Henrietta—to look and feel like a fairy queen on her wedding day. Unfortunately Henrietta was detained in the library with work and would miss the unveiling of the doll dressed in the lemon yellow. She would make sure it was carefully displayed on the pier table.

Amelia's heart thrummed a nervous beat, and her stomach had a flock of butterflies flitting around. In one look, Amelia would know if her vision meshed with Gwyneth's imagined dress, or if she'd have to bury her own feelings and start again.

Gwyneth's dark, slanted eyes filled with tears. "She is beautiful. I couldn't have dreamed a more wonderful gown."

She watched Gwyneth gulp and shiver with excitement. Relief washed through Amelia. She let out the breath she had been holding in anticipation of this moment.

"With your dramatic looks, I envisioned you as a medieval Madonna."

Gwyneth gave a teary giggle. "Me, a Madonna?"

"A veil with the red crown is simple but more dramatic than a bonnet. And the red crown is vivid and will highlight your dark eyes and hair."

Gwyneth stared at the doll in her lap touching the miniscule veil. "I want to look beautiful for Ash. But that you had the vision and knew what I'd like is incomprehensible." Gwyneth squeezed her hand. "Amelia, you are so very talented and so very dear to me."

She felt a bit embarrassed by Gwyneth's fervent display. "I've selected the perfect fabrics and will need you to come with me…"

The door to the morning room flew open as Edward and Gus rushed in. "Are you almost done? I'm finished with my lessons and ready for today's match."

Gus ran toward the women in pursuit of the food on the tea tray sitting on the table in front of the settee. Spurred on by his Labrador's love of food, Gus raced toward the table. He held his nose high in the air for a scent of meat or other delectable. Gus was not picky.

"We are to meet after tea, following Uncle Charles' and Henrietta's nap," Gwyneth said.

Amelia was accustomed to her own younger brother's impatience, especially around sports. "Why don't you go set up the equipment? I'll come out, and we can practice before everyone else assembles." Amelia avoided the thought that everyone would include Lord Brinsley.

"Great! I'll get the equipment with Mr. Marlow." Edward scooped up two biscuits from the tray before leaving.

"That was very sweet of you, Amelia. I know Edward is feeling a bit lost with Henrietta's pregnancy and my obligations with the wedding."

Amelia paid no attention to Gus chewing on a prize he had snatched from the table.

Amelia stood. "I'll need you to accompany me to Madame de Puis'. I've selected fabric that I think will be perfect, but, of course, you'll need to decide."

Amelia picked up the silk scrap to rewrap the dolls. She bent to the table where the second doll had lain. The doll was gone. Panic punched through her body. She stared at the table as if she couldn't comprehend that the doll wasn't where she had placed it.

She looked under the table, and there was Gus with the doll in his mouth. Not chewing, but holding—like a prized possession.

"Oh, no! Gus has the doll," Amelia shouted. "Gus, drop that, now." She rushed around the table to grab the doll out of Gus' slobbering mouth. How would she ever explain to Helene?

Gus immediately assumed that Amelia wanted to play the game of keep-away as he did with Edward. Gus bolted toward the door; fortunately it was closed.

Gwyneth jumped up to assist in the chase. Both women ran at the dog, who dodged them and ran around the settee then between the tables.

Amelia couldn't breathe. Gwyneth screeched, "Drop, Gus." The command had no effect on the dog, who had retreated under Henrietta's morning desk.

The dog stretched out on his stomach with one paw on the doll. He looked at them from underneath the lady's desk, his chocolate brown eyes soft and playful.

"We have to get the doll from him before he eats it." Amelia couldn't restrain the sheer panic in her voice.

"He won't eat it. Labs like soft toys because of their hunting mouths." Gwyneth tried to sound consoling, but she too was worried. This was no toy, but an expensive item belonging to a valued friend.

Amelia and Gwyneth walked slowly to the desk, trying to avoid encouraging the dog to start the game again. Amelia dropped to her knees in front of the desk, and projected her most imperious voice, the one that always worked when her brothers were ill-behaved. "Gus, give me the doll."

By now, the doll was well back in the dog's mouth. Amelia's stomach churned, imagining the damage to the irreplaceable doll. She reached beyond the clenched jaws, grabbed the doll, and pulled. Gus who thought it was a new game of tug of war, pulled back and the porcelain head of the doll broke off in Amelia's hand. Sparkly jewels spilled from the doll's head and scattered on the rug.

"Oh, no," Amelia sobbed.

Gus, who finally seemed to recognize Amelia's distress, dropped the rest of the doll.

Amelia touched the sparkling jewels that had spilled out of the doll's head.

Gwyneth dropped to her knees next to Amelia. "Are those diamonds?"

Both women sat on the floor with Gus watching them avidly, hoping for yet another game. Amelia retrieved the doll's body from Gus' reach. There was no damage to the doll itself, but she wasn't sure the silk had fared so well.

Gwyneth held one of the jewels up to the light. "It's a diamond, and a very beautiful one at that. Why would Madame de Puis put diamonds in her dolls?"

A terrible sick sensation shot through Amelia. Helene didn't make the dolls. They were smuggled from France. Could Helene be part of a smuggling ring?

Amelia inspected the inside of the head. There were no more diamonds in the small cavity.

Gwyneth gathered up the diamonds in a pile. "I've counted twelve—a fortune."

"You know what this means?" Amelia couldn't disguise the fear in her voice.

"Madame de Puis is a smuggler." Gwyneth finished the forbidding thought aloud.

"That is preposterous." Although Amelia had already considered the idea, she'd rejected the possibility that her friend was a criminal. "Surely Helene would never do anything illegal."

"But you've told me she gets her fabrics from smugglers."

"Yes, but...I just don't believe she's otherwise involved. I don't think she knows what was in the heads. Why would she lend the dolls to me if they contained a fortune?"

Amelia gathered up the diamonds and the doll's head and body and slowly climbed to her feet.

Gwyneth did likewise. "Are you able to get the head back on?"

"Yes, it fits easily back into the body." Amelia twisted the porcelain head back into the body. Neither Gwyneth nor Amelia could admire the doll anymore, now it had become something disreputable.

"Should we look in the other doll's head?" asked Gwyneth.

Amelia nodded in agreement. Her thoughts rushed in a mix of logic and emotion. She had to protect her friend. Helene would be punished ferociously if she was caught in any association with a French smuggling ring; it was bad enough that she bought goods from a smuggler. With Napoleon ready to invade England, anti-French feelings and suspicions were running high.

Gwyneth held the doll in its gorgeous lemon yellow dress. "Do you want to do this, or shall I?"

Overwhelmed, Amelia nodded. "You can do it."

Amelia and Gwyneth sat down on the settee together. Gwyneth slowly turned the head out of the body. She held the doll over her lap in the smooth part of her skirt. Again, diamonds spilled out. This time Amelia counted. Twelve small but perfect diamonds. What had Helene gotten into?

"Are you going to tell Helene what you've found?"

"I'm trying to decide the best approach."

"But if you tell her and she knows, that makes her a criminal; you could be in serious danger."

"I don't believe it. I can't believe it," Amelia said adamantly, desperate to convince herself as much as Gwyneth. She thought of the long hours with Helene, pouring over fabrics, drawings, sharing their love of fashion.

"I agree. I can't imagine Madame de Puis as a threat. Maybe

we should put the diamonds back and not tell her," Gwyneth said.

"But what will that accomplish?"

"We could return the dolls and see who comes for them. Someone knows about the diamonds. Someone will want them. And if Helene is involved, we'll know."

Amelia recognized the excitement in Gwyneth's voice and the way her dark eyes lightened. Gwyneth was primed for an adventure.

"I'm not sure I'm following your plan." Amelia was committed to do whatever would help her friend, a French émigré who had worked hard to survive after the French terror. Amelia's father was well placed in society and government; he could help if Helene needed protection.

"You spend a great deal of time at the shop. And with my wedding, I'll need to be there for fittings," Gwyneth continued, immersed in her plans of a real spy adventure.

"But how does that help us know about the dolls."

"We can observe the people who come and go. We can do what Ash and Brinsley did last night. They went undercover to a pub on the docks, to observe."

"I've spent a great deal of time in the shop and the only people who frequent the shop are ladies of the ton or gentlemen with their paramours."

"Yes, I know, but I'm talking about the back of the shop. Who delivers the fabrics?"

Amelia smiled at Gwyneth. "You are really good at this spy stuff."

Gwyneth grinned back in her infectious way; it made both of them laugh.

Then Amelia had a thought. "What about Ash?"

"What about Ash?" Gwyneth's chin went out in a mulish manner familiar to Amelia.

"Helene is my friend and I want to help her, but I don't want to cause any problems between you and Ash. You don't have to be involved."

"I *want* to be involved. Wedding planning is fun, but I don't have your talent in the design. My talent is in spy work. I come from a family of spies."

Amelia knew Cord was a spy, but who else did Gwyneth mean?

"We're going to only do the leg-work, as Cord calls it. And if we need help, we can ask my Aunt Euphemia," Gwyneth said.

"Your Aunt Euphemia? She's dear, but I can't see her helping."

"You don't know about Aunt Euphemia? I thought Henrietta would've told you. My Aunt Euphemia was, and most likely still is, a spy, even though she would deny it."

"Your Aunt Euphemia is what?"

"A spy." Gwyneth's dark eyes twinkled.

"A spy? Really?"

Gwyneth laughed. "Is there an echo in here? Yes, my aunt helped rescue women and children from France during the Reign of Terror. If Aunt Euphemia can help women escape France, you and I can help one French woman already in England."

"When you put it that way, I agree…to help Helene."

"Tomorrow, we'll return the dolls. You said I had to come and see the fabric. We can ask a few questions."

Why was her stomach roiling and her skin chilled while Gwyneth, with her wide smile and twinkling eyes, was clearly blooming with excitement over her next great adventure?

"Once we know that Helene isn't involved. And when we know who is smuggling diamonds, then we'll tell Ash and Cord," Gwyneth said, certain of her plan.

Everything always sounded fine when Gwyneth was excited about it, but it did nothing to settle the dread growing in Amelia's stomach.

"Let's get these diamonds back into the dolls before Edward comes for you."

The only good part of the morning—she had nearly forgotten—she now faced a cricket game that included Lord Brinsley.

CHAPTER SIX

Brinsley and Ashworth sat in front of Lord Rathbourne's desk, a brandy glass in hand. Brinsley felt accepted in the inner circle. After last night's punch-up, he had moved up in Ash's estimation. Men were uncomplicated—a good fight shared, and their friendship was sealed. Perhaps Ash had done him a favor warning him against Amelia.

"We followed the only man who ran out of the tavern. He went to a flat on the border of St. Giles. I have Talley and his men watching. We'll monitor his comings and goings. He must be very low in the business by the look of his rooms," Ash said. "But he was the only one who got very nervous when the brawl broke out."

"There is no question that the French have more than one man working there," Brinsley said. "There were several men who avoided the fight. The men enjoying the fracas were definitely the dock workers."

"Good work, gentlemen." Rathbourne leaned forward over his desk and smirked at his good friend. "By the way, Ash, did you start the brawl for old time's sake since you're about to become a married man?"

Brinsley wanted to ask Ash the same question. Hell, Ashworth wasn't sporting a black eye to reinforce his rakish reputation with a certain lady.

Ashworth snorted. "I'm not grieving the loss of tavern fights. Any loss of my past life's adventures can't compare with my future with Gwyneth."

Rathbourne leaned back against his chair and crossed his arms. "Just like you, Ash, to emerge unscathed. Brinsley got mangled while you came out without a scratch. Back in the day when Ash and I would get into a good brawl… Oh, God, I'm starting to sound like a stodgy old man, reminiscing about our fights."

Ash leaned back in his chair, crossing one leg over the other. "I really didn't start the fracas because it was my last mission before the wedding. I needed a distraction. I wanted to see who would scatter once the mayhem started. There were two workmen whose hands didn't look like they had ever done a day of manual work. Clearly, they were watching Brinsley. I'm not sure what they intended, but I knew that establishing Brinsley as a fearless fighter would help his cover."

Rathbourne inspected Brinsley's shiner. "I'm sorry Brinsley, but I'm glad the bridegroom didn't take this shot. Gwyneth would have my hide if anything happened to his mug."

Brinsley wanted to explain that he had never been taken by surprise in a fight before, but he didn't want to sound like he was losing his edge.

"Cord, you should've seen Brinsley. He has the same flair for a fight as you do. He taunted a bruiser who definitely was the strong arm of the place. I swear he was the size of a Goliath, and Brinsley called him a 'damn coward.' The look on the giant's face was worth another evening waiting in a seedy tavern. Brinsley took the guy down so quickly that he'll be well remembered. He also made a contact for himself," Ash said with relish.

"A woman?" Rathbourne raised his eyebrows.

Brinsley cleared his throat, his first contribution to the conversation. "She's a tavern wench who is willing to keep an eye out for my drunk brother who likes to pretend he's French."

"Let me check her out before you make further contact. What's her name?" Cord asked.

"All I got was Bev, before Ash started the ruckus." Brinsley tried to keep the antagonism out of his voice. Ash's reasons were sound, but next time he'd like to have some warning before all hell broke loose.

Rathbourne gave him a look of appreciation. "That's good. Bev witnessed the fight?"

"I assume so, but I only had time to fend off attacks then catch up with Ash. I never reconnected with her."

"Nicely played." Rathbourne nodded.

Brinsley's chest eased. The two highly respected men didn't intimidate him, but their approval meant a lot to him.

"Do you think Bev could be working both sides?"

"Most likely, but she was very accommodating when I threw the French part at her."

Ash snorted. "Yes, she did look very accommodating."

Brinsley felt uncertain about how to react to this new camaraderie from Ash.

"Another reason for Ash, on the verge of marriage, not to be on site in this operation," Rathbourne said.

Ash chuckled. "Lady Henrietta had a lot of difficulty accepting Cord's relationship with one of his female informants."

Rathbourne ran his fingers through his thick shock of dark hair, a nervous habit that Brinsley was starting to recognize. "Yes, it is one of the many pitfalls of our work."

Rathbourne gave Ash a piercing, black look that would send anyone into hiding, but Ash was unaffected. "I guess that's one way of describing the circles Lady Henrietta had you running in."

"This is the problem of having friends working for you. They forget their rank." Rathbourne shook his head.

This comment made Ash laugh even louder.

Rathbourne ignored Ash and focused on Brinsley. "Now that you've been accepted into Lady Henrietta's and Lady Gwyneth's circle, you'll have to be very circumspect about this mission, especially around my sister. She is always looking for adventure. She believes spying runs in the blood."

Brinsley raised an eyebrow. "Will do, sir."

Ash grew serious. "Gwyneth will not be involved in any further missions. Her involvement in the Christmas party was a total fluke. If I hadn't been poisoned, she never would've been involved."

Rathbourne grunted. "Spoken like a man who hasn't been married yet."

"I'm certain marriage to me will be enough of an adventure for Gwyneth." Ash took a large gulp of his drink.

"Damn, Ash. I don't want to hear this about my sister. Rathbourne held up his glass. "Top me off."

"Sorry old man." Ash stood and poured brandy into Rathbourne's empty glass.

"Brinsley, what were your impressions of *Ship's Aground*?"

Brinsley sat up in his chair. "I agree with Lord Ashworth."

Ash turned in his seat and looked at Brinsley. "You don't have to 'lord' me after the Christmas party and now our brawl. Call me Ash."

Brinsley nodded. "There are French there amongst the workers. During the brawl, you could hear the French cussing. I didn't see any money being exchanged during my brief stint in the tavern." Brinsley took a sip of brandy. "But how do we know the French haven't already infiltrated the Navy yard?"

"I've had a man inside the shipyard since the project started." Rathbourne shuffled the papers on his desk. "Nothing suspicious has been reported."

"You sly dog, Cord," Ash said.

"I wasn't going to wait on the Navy to tell me when they wanted our involvement." Lord Rathbourne stood. "Brinsley, I'll expect regular updates on the business at *Ship's Aground*. You can report to Ash, and when it's necessary, we'll speak."

"Yes, sir. I'll begin my surveillance tonight."

"The secret weapon will be ready for testing in one week's time." Lord Rathbourne walked toward the expansive windows looking out over the garden. "Now it's time to play cricket. I've promised Edward that you'll play as well, Brinsley. It seems Edward is quite impressed with your size. He's convinced that with you and Miss Amelia on his side, he'll be able to beat us old men."

Ash draped his arm over the back of the chair in an insolent manner. "Cord, you can't actually be worried that we could be beaten by a child and a woman?"

From his seat, Brinsley could see that young Edward and his tutor were setting up the wickets. He had pretended that he didn't anticipate this morning. The idea of participating with this group, doing something ordinary, was beyond imagination. He had endured four years since he'd been rejected by society for his supposed scandalous behavior toward his brother's fiancée. Disgraced, he had been ostracized by society until his work as an agent brought him into Lord Rathbourne's circle.

"Oh, I'm confident we will win. We've experience on our side." Ash looked right at Brinsley.

Another challenge thrown down by Ash—but, of course, he didn't know that Brinsley and his brother grew up playing cricket, and with his size and strength, he made a damn good bowler.

Lord Rathbourne looked at Brinsley, his eyebrows raised. "I'm aware of your strength in fights, but you'll need to show us your speed."

Lord Rathbourne believed his size slowed him down. Well, wouldn't his superior be surprised?

Ash leered at Brinsley. "I admire Edward for his choice of teammates, another brilliant Harcourt in the making. Brinsley is an unknown factor, but Edward has decided his size will be in his favor. The teammate I'd want is Miss Amelia. Never seen a better wicket keeper. If she weren't a woman…"

Brinsley moved uncomfortably in his seat. He wasn't sure what upset him more—the idea that Ash wanted Amelia on his team or the way Ash said she was a woman. Brinsley was damn glad she was a woman. Happier than he should be by far.

Ash now looked at him as if he could read every one of his lustful thoughts.

"I guess we'll have to see how the game goes." Brinsley

wasn't a man prone to bragging. He was a man of action, and he was confident that he could beat Lord Rathbourne and Ash. He wasn't sure if they were egging him on to prove his worth or if it was the basic male need to compete.

Lord Rathbourne waved his hand in dismissal. "You both go ahead. I've more work to finish before I can join you."

Brinsley and Ash stood together.

"I've told Gwyneth that I'd wait for her once she was finished with Amelia," Ash said.

Brinsley hated the way his heart accelerated at the sound of her name, more so knowing that she was already in the house.

"I'll go out and help young Edward with the setup."

Ash walked out with him. "You're a good man to have around, Brinsley." With that, Ash turned and headed down the hall to the morning room where the ladies were working. Brinsley wished he could go in search of Amelia, but it was a lot safer to help Edward.

CHAPTER SEVEN

Brinsley took a deep breath, savoring the crisp January afternoon air. Anticipating the sight of Miss Amelia Bonnington playing cricket in breeches, his heart thumped against his chest and his body thrummed with nervous energy.

He rounded the corner to find Amelia squatting in front of the wicket. She had her back to him so he was able to enjoy the enticing view. She hadn't worn breeches, but he wasn't disappointed. The muslin, pulled tightly against her rounded derriere, revealed enough to send a blast of heat through his body as if he were a billowing furnace.

He couldn't stop staring. Unaware of his presence, she shifted her weight. He moaned aloud from the lust licking along his spine. He had never before experienced any woman who could fire him up in an instant. And he was definitely up.

Gus, who had been quietly chewing on a stick, was the first to spot him or hear his moan. Had he really moaned aloud? The dog dropped his stick and raced toward him.

Edward, oblivious to his dog, but just as eager, ran over too. "This is capital. We can practice before the others arrive."

Amelia quickly turned and stood with Edward's greeting. Her skirt was divided like a riding garment, but the thin fabric made it looked like she wore undergarments. The sunlight was behind her revealing the outline of her long, shapely legs through the translucent, white fabric. His heart beat erratically and his breaths came in short bursts. This innocent woman would be the death of him.

"Lord Brinsley." Her voice was as formal as if they were meeting in the drawing room, as if she was totally unaware that her choice of dress did nothing to hide her lithe body and lovely legs.

He forced himself to divert his gaze and look up at her face. "Miss Amelia." He bowed carefully.

"Oh, my goodness." Her eyes were wide with shock.

God, had she noticed his uncontrollable physical reaction to her state of dishabille.

"Your face." Had his out of control fantasies shown on his face?

"It must hurt." Her soft voice was filled with concern.

What the hell?

As she got close enough for him to see the blue speckles in her violet eyes, her brows knotted together. "You were in a fight?"

Her disapproval suddenly turned sunny into cold and lonely. He wasn't able to disclose his mission. And why should he care what she thought of him. She had already pronounced that he wasn't worthy husband material.

"I was in a tavern brawl."

He had expected her to respond with disgust, but instead her face and lips softened in understanding, as if she knew him better than he did himself. "I'm sorry."

Edward hurried over after abandoning his task with the wickets and had a very different reaction to news of the fight. "Wow, I'd like to see what you did to the other guy. You flattened him, didn't you?"

"That's enough, Edward." Amelia treated Edward as if he were her younger brother. She appeared very comfortable in her role as older sister.

"Is this the new fashion for women cricketers?" He couldn't stop himself from staring at her legs. "You look ready to play cricket." What a pile of... She looked ready for a long hard tumble.

She smiled sunnily, which only made matters worse. Her

eyes sparkled with amusement, tantalizing him, robbing him of conscious thought. "This is a gown I've designed to help my movement in the game. With long skirts gowns and petticoats, how could I be expected to play my position as wicket keeper?"

The idea of "her position" fired his carnal thoughts. The only position he could think of was her under him. He would've laughed if every muscle in his body weren't tightened and primed. He adjusted his jacket, trying to conceal his reaction. He couldn't stop staring at her outfit. He had never seen a respectable lady in such a get-up. He had seen many women in various stages of undress, but Amelia in this costume caught his blood on fire.

"Sir, with you on our team we can't lose." Edward looked up at him in awe.

At least he could still impress children. "Well, I'd hope so since I have it on the best authority that Miss Amelia is the finest wicket keeper in all of England."

Amelia's soft lips curved into a self-deprecating smirk. "Edward has a very generous opinion of my skills."

"Ash also spoke highly of your skills. He believes if you weren't a woman, you'd be one of the best."

She laughed and dismissed Ash's compliment with a wave of her graceful hand. "Fiddlesticks. I'm a wicket keeper. Is shouldn't matter that I'm a woman."

Her laughter shot straight through him, ratcheting his readiness. It mattered to him greatly that she was a woman.

Edward grabbed the ball. "Amelia, can we get back to practice? Lord Brinsley can help me with my bowling."

She continued to smile. "If that is amenable to Lord Brinsley."

She was different today, not fighting him as if he were the enemy and not rejecting the obvious attraction between them. "If we are to be teammates then I think you both should call me Derrick. My close friends all call me Derrick."

He watched her color change instantaneously from porcelain white to rosy pink. When he had been desperate for her, he asked her to call him Derrick. Her breathlessness when she uttered his name was imprinted in his brain. If he had to suffer endless torment, then she might as well suffer a little too. Not exactly the behavior of a gentleman, but she didn't think of him as a gentleman anyway.

Edward, his blond curls ruffled by the wind, handed Brinsley the ball. The young boy's enthusiasm was hard to ignore. "Before everyone arrives, can we get to my bowling?" Edward kicked at the grass, not looking at him. Gus waited next to the boy on full alert. "I'd rather not practice in front of everyone else."

"I'd be happy to help you." A cricket bowl thrown over-the-shoulder, with a complete straight arm, required strength and agility. Brinsley could understand why Edward, at such a young age, might be self-conscious. But with hard work, Edward would make a fine bowler someday. By the fierce, burning light in Edward's face, the boy wouldn't want to hear that he had to wait until he was older. "I find the trickiest part of the bowl is keeping the arm straight in the release."

Edward looked at him as if his words were the Holy Grail. "Will you watch me bowl to Amelia?"

Amelia smiled at Edward and went to pick up the bat. She planted her legs in a wide stance and got into striker position with the bat held at the ready. Her splayed and bent posture was perfect for flexibility, but it wasn't the flexibility of a striker that Brinsley envisioned. She looked up and smiled widely at Edward. "I'm ready."

With a face locked in concentration, Edward stood behind the bowling crease. He wound up, lunged forward, and threw the ball. His timing was jerky as he franticly struggled to cover the distance between the bowling crease and the popping crease. And, of course, his ultimate goal was to throw the ball really fast.

Amelia swung the bat athletically and gracefully. He'd never be able to play cricket again without envisioning Amelia, her skirt swishing around her legs, totally absorbed in trying to hit the ball. Edward's bowl went wide making it impossible for her to connect.

Amelia scurried to pick up the ball and walk it back to Edward. "You got nervous in front of Lord Brinsley. Shall we give it another go?"

Crestfallen at his poor performance, Edward shook his head. "I'm horrible as a bowler."

"I don't agree," said Brinsley. "I think there are things we can work on." Amelia, who had been focused on Edward, looked up at him and beamed. Her radiant face jolted his heart into a frantic race. He cleared his throat, trying to look away.

"I think you need to slow down your pitch. Let's work on accuracy today and not speed. Miss Amelia, can you take your position again?"

She nodded and resumed her spot. The sunlight reflected the shades of red—glimpses of molten fire in her hair. He tracked every one of her movements as if mesmerized.

She turned back and spoke over her shoulder. "Edward, remember to release your breath as you release the ball. It really helps."

"What excellent advice." His voice must have sounded incredulous.

She laughed as she bent to retrieve the bat. "You needn't act so shocked."

He smiled at her, caught in her magic. He felt like a young boy himself. He hadn't felt this young and alive since before the whole disaster with his brother.

Edward stood tense, fingering the ball in his hand.

"Let me watch you slowly go through your entire bowl."

Edward nodded. "I'll try."

Edward lunged too far forward for his size, probably mimicking the throw of a larger man.

"Let's have you take a smaller step before you throw the ball. Can you try it?"

"Okay." Edward took a smaller step, but his timing was still off, with is attempt to throw the ball hard and fast, his release was too late. The ball bounced on the ground and rolled.

"Give me another one, Edward. Keeping trying," Amelia chimed.

Edward was a fine athlete with a great focus and in no time would progress rapidly, but still a young boy. He was too self-conscious for this kind of close scrutiny.

"Keep bowling to Miss Amelia. I'll play the wicket keeper."

Amelia, sensing Edward's nervousness, spoke to him in a chipper voice. "Come on, Edward, let's show Lord Brinsley how we plan to beat those lazybones who aren't out here yet."

Edward smiled, his first since he had started his demonstration.

Brinsley moved behind Amelia and took position as wicket keeper.

Amelia whispered, "Thank you for taking the time to practice with him." She looked into his eyes with appreciation. Her admiring look coiled his guts in painful pleasure.

He couldn't stop looking at her bright eyes and flushed cheeks. He hadn't been close to goodness in a very long time. A warmness enveloped his heart, making him feel young and hopeful. "I'm more impressed that a lady with so many responsibilities for the wedding is taking time to play with a young boy."

"With four brothers, I understand boys. And Henrietta isn't feeling well enough to give Edward the attention he needs."

"Are you ready to play?" Edward asked impatiently.

Brinsley squatted into his wicket keeper position behind the striker.

"Yes, of course." Amelia got into her striker stance, her sweet derriere pointed right at his face.

He tried to focus on Edward, but he couldn't stop looking at the view. "My God." He swore under his breath and moaned.

Amelia turned toward him. "Pardon me?"

Amelia never saw the ball coming at her. Edward had finally coordinated his bowl, making his pitch more accurate and much faster. Of all the times for him to finally get it right. The heavy ball hit Amelia squarely on the side of her head. She gasped and fell sprawling to the ground.

Brinsley dropped to his knees beside her. Blood trickled from the wound on the side of her head. How could he have allowed injury to come to this lovable woman? Agony crushed the air from his lungs.

Edward ran toward them. "Amelia. I didn't mean to hit you."

Gus, who had been under a tree chewing on a stick, jumped up and ran to Amelia. He lay next to her, licking her hand.

"Edward, go into the house and tell Lady Gwyneth that Amelia is hurt." Panic laced Brinsley's voice.

"But, but…I didn't mean to hurt her. She never gets hit. She is so fast."

"It wasn't your fault. I distracted her."

Relief washed across Edward's face. "You were talking to her in the middle of the bowl?"

Brinsley nodded. He gently pushed her hair away to assess the damage. The cut wasn't deep, but head wounds always bleed profusely. Her pale skin made the crimson blood look more ominous. He took out his handkerchief and pressed it to the laceration.

"Edward, go. Alert Lady Gwyneth. We'll need a doctor." His voice echoed in his ears.

He lifted Amelia into his arms, holding her soft body tight against his chest. It was all his fault. If he hadn't been distracting her, she would've seen the ball coming.

His emotions were a lethal mix of regret and tenderness.

"I'm sorry," he whispered as he carried her to the house.

He stared down at her white face. Her thick lashes shadowed her cheeks. Her loosened hair, the color of fire, hung over his arms.

The motion of his brisk pace jarred Amelia. She stirred in his arms then opened her eyes and stared at him.

"Amelia?"

She touched her cold hand to his face. "Why did you fight?"

Her touch was gentle and tentative, but the slight caress went deep into his body and into his empty soul. "What?"

She had been knocked out, her head was bleeding, and she wanted to know about his fight. "Amelia, do you remember that you got hit in the head with the cricket ball?"

"Edward must be getting better. I didn't see it coming."

Remorse and guilt weighed heavily upon him. "I distracted you."

She searched his face. "Why would you do that?"

"I'm so sorry. I'll never forgive myself. Do you have a headache?"

"A little bit. Not the worst cricket injury I've had."

He climbed the steps from the garden to the terrace as Lady Gwyneth rushed out of the French doors. "Amelia. Are you hurt?"

Amelia turned her head. "I'm fine, Gwyneth."

Lady Gwyneth took Amelia's hand into her own. "Thank God, you're awake. Edward said you were unconscious."

"She was knocked out for a moment, and she's got a nasty cut on her head. Did you send for the doctor?"

"You're so pale," Lady Gwyneth said.

"I'm always pale." Amelia chuckled. "A red-head's blight."

"How can you joke at a time like this?" Lady Gwyneth asked. "Your hands are like ice."

"I'll be fine once someone attends to my cut. And I'm sure I can walk." She looked up at Brinsley. "You can put me down now."

"You're not walking up all those stairs." Lady Gwyneth pulled her hand back and said in an imperious voice, "Follow me." She led them down the hallway to the stairwell. "We'll take her to my bedroom."

The butler rushed up to them. "Miss Amelia, I'm glad to see you awake. Mrs. Brompton is assembling supplies to take care of your wound."

"Thank you, Brompton. I'm sorry to be a problem for you and the Mrs."

"You're never a problem, Miss Amelia." The butler bowed.

"Brompton, where is Edward?" Lady Gwyneth asked.

"Lady Rathbourne is with him. He is quite shaken by the accident."

Amelia reached out and put her hand on Gwyneth's arm. "I need to tell him it wasn't his fault. I wasn't looking."

"You weren't looking? That doesn't sound like you." Lady Gwyneth raised her eyebrows and looked directly at Brinsley.

"It was entirely my fault. I spoke to Miss Amelia during the bowl," he said.

Lady Gwyneth's eyes narrowed in speculation. "Mmm…"

He felt burning on the top of his ears. He hadn't blushed since he was a child.

Lady Gwyneth patted Amelia's arm. "You can tell Edward after we've cleaned your wound. Right now, you'd scare the poor child. You're a mess."

Amelia and Lady Gwyneth giggled.

Brinsley couldn't share their mirth. He hated feeling helpless and guilty.

"Thank you, Brompton," Lady Gwyneth said. "Right this way, Lord Brinsley."

CHAPTER EIGHT

As Amelia leaned back against the pillow, her head ached and the bandage felt too tight. Surprisingly she was in a cheerful mood, remembering Lord Brinsley's gentle touch and the warmth and security she felt while pressed against his chest.

There was a light tap on the door, followed by Gwyneth entering. "How are you feeling?"

"I'm absolutely fine and a bit embarrassed. I'm not seriously injured. There is really no need for such a fuss."

"Why would you be embarrassed that you got hit by a ball?" Gwyneth sat on the edge of the bed.

"Because good players don't get caught unaware. They move out of the way of the ball. This injury will convince the men that women do not belong on the field."

"Can women play as well as men?" Gwyneth asked. "You're the first woman I know who plays. I mean really plays."

"Probably not, because of the difference in size and strength of women versus men. But don't tell the gentleman that I admitted to such heresy." Amelia giggled.

"You're in a very good mood for taking a hit to the head." Gwyneth's chocolate eyes sparkled with mischief.

"I'm fine. Everyone is making such a big deal about a simple knock."

"Not everyone. In fact, just one person…Brinsley." Gwyneth's grin grew broader.

Amelia felt the familiar heat moving from her stomach to her chest to her face at the mention of his name.

"You poor dear." Gwyneth smiled sympathetically. "You can never hide your feelings when your face turns the color of a tomato."

"Is this your bedside manner? It's surprising that Ash survived your care-giving."

Gwyneth sniggered. "I'm sorry, but you do turn the most amazing shades of red."

"Yes, as my obnoxious brothers have pointed out to me my entire life."

"I'm looking forward to meeting those hellions at the ball next week. Are they all red-heads?"

"I'm the only true red-head, but Drew and Jack have red highlights. Parker and Colin are more blond than red."

"But back to your problem—a very virile and very handsome problem."

"I've no idea what you're talking about."

She hadn't fooled Gwyneth for a second, judging by the determined gleam in her eyes.

"You're going to pretend you didn't notice the possessive way Brinsley carried you? The man was in agony every time you winced. If it weren't painful to watch, it would've been comical seeing a man his size looking like a repentant young boy caught in some trouble."

The memory of his tender touch, his heat, and the scent of musk and maleness were doing strange things to her body.

Gwyneth smiled again. "Exactly what I thought."

"Do not say another word. I still haven't forgiven you for meddling and having Ash speak to Lord Brinsley on my behalf."

"I never asked Ash to speak to him." Gwyneth held her hand to her chest. "I swear."

"All right, I believe you. But you mustn't do anything else. No secret plans. No meddling!"

"Speaking of secret plans. Are you well enough to go to Madame de Puis' tomorrow?"

Amelia didn't miss that Gwyneth hadn't agreed to refrain

from interfering or meddling. "Of course, I'm fine. I wouldn't miss returning the dolls for anything."

"I'm so glad to have an adventure. Ash and Brinsley are working on something that neither Cord nor Ash will reveal to me. They have both told me it's safer for me not to know." Gwyneth's looked down and ran her finger over the pattern in the heavy damask bedcover. "I thought, after the Christmas party, Ash would be more amenable to sharing his missions."

"With the impending invasion of England, everyone is more fearful and guarded. I can understand why the men are acting the way they are."

Gwyneth's head jerked up. "You can?"

"I understand their instinct to want to protect us. But I wish they saw us as capable of helping. My cricket playing is a perfect example. The men can't believe that I'm proficient in catching and throwing a ball, and now they will believe they are right."

"Well, we're going to show them when we identify the smugglers and figure out their plans," Gwyneth gushed. "Maybe, with this case, Ash will finally believe I can be a helpmate."

"He's so in love with you. I don't think he's going to want you involved with smugglers."

"Don't say that, Amelia. I'll start feeling guilty about our little adventure. And speaking of guilty, Brinsley is waiting to apologize."

Amelia's heart thrummed against her chest. "He doesn't need to apologize."

"Please, Amelia, put the man out of his misery. He looks as if he's ready for the gallows. He's pacing in the library and pleaded with me to see you when you felt up to it."

"Fine, but I look a mess."

"You do." Gwyneth laughed heartily as she made her way to the door. She turned back and spoke over her shoulder. "The man is so in love with you, he won't notice that your head is wrapped in a bandage and your face is blotchy and turning your favorite color—purple."

CHAPTER NINE

Amelia didn't share Gwyneth's amusement. She wanted to believe that Lord Brinsley cared about her, but who could rely on the opinion of a blissful bride? She wished she wasn't lying in bed like an invalid with her tangled hair and a bandage wrapped around her head, but Gwyneth was adamant she had to remain recumbent. Doctor's orders.

Gwyneth opened the door with the sound of the footman's tap and waved in the visitor.

"Brinsley. Please come and see for yourself that the patient is doing fine."

Gwyneth waited at the door, as Lord Brinsley entered. His brown, curly hair was tousled; his shirt and cravat were stained with blood. His eyes were dark and sunken with anxiety.

Amelia had been unaware of the tenderness she felt for him until now; she wanted to hold him, to comfort him, but she didn't dare.

"Thank you, Lady Gwyneth." Brinsley's voice and manner were much subdued.

Gwyneth curtsied to the gentleman and left the room, closing the door behind her.

Amelia clenched her hands on the damask coverlet. She'd be scolding Gwyneth for this newest attempt at matchmaking. Gwyneth's maid was in the dressing room a few yards away, but Gwyneth had left her alone with Lord Brinsley.

He edged closer to the bed, scrutinizing her face, noting details of the bandage and the facial swelling.

"Miss Amelia, are you comfortable?" His voice was hoarse with emotion.

She tried to lighten his serious mood. "My injury doesn't warrant bed rest, but Lady Gwyneth and the doctor were quite fearsome."

"Of course, you must rest. You lost a great deal of blood, and you're quite pale."

"I doubt greatly that I'm pale. This is my normal skin color. I suspect you look worse than I do." There was purple bruising below his eye, covering his strong cheekbone almost back to his ear. "I stopped a ball, but by the looks of it, you stopped a very large fist. We make quite a pair; now we're matching." She teased, but the gorgeous man stared at her as if she were on her deathbed.

He stepped closer and she got a whiff of his scent—lime and male muskiness. "I'm truly sorry. This was my fault. If I had stayed quiet, you wouldn't be injured."

The way he looked at her, with such concern and care, she couldn't look away. Butterflies danced a fast tempo in her stomach. She was captured again in his all-consuming stare.

He clasped her hand gently, as if cradling a flower. Growing up with brothers, she had never been treated delicately. "That you could've been seriously injured will always weigh on me."

This man couldn't be the rogue he was reputed to be. He was gentle and caring. The heat of his hand and his total attentiveness was causing her heart to thump in irregular beats against her night rail. "Please, you mustn't berate yourself. I've had much worse injuries from playing cricket with my brothers. My brothers are hell-raisers, and if they were here, they wouldn't believe I was in bed over a minor knock on the head."

"Your brothers should be horse-whipped for mistreating you. I'd never hurt you or want to see you hurt." He leaned closer as if to kiss her.

Amelia couldn't force air into her lungs. Her mouth was dry, and she licked her lips.

He watched her tongue, entranced. He withdrew his hand to

his side. "Miss Amelia, is there anything I can do to make amends?"

Feeling heady from this enormous male's devouring stare and intense attention, she contemplated his riveted concern. "I want to know what you said before I got hit with the ball."

His eyes widened in surprise and his posture stiffened.

Her curiosity grew. Whatever he had said, he was obviously hesitant to share.

"What I said isn't important. I was wrong to distract you."

"You did ask what I needed." Bantering with the serious and very attractive Lord Brinsley was definitely helping her headache. "What did you say?"

The golden chips in his green eyes darkened. He opened his mouth, then closed it without speaking.

Definitely an interesting reaction. She couldn't untangle her own reaction to the dazzling man. Interacting with Lord Brinsley was challenging and stimulating. She wanted to tease him and comfort him at the same time. He looked desperate for tenderness.

"Your silence makes the remark more interesting and mysterious. I love mysteries. I won't let you escape until you tell me." She used her charming voice—the one that usually could soften her brothers and her father.

"It isn't a mystery." He stared at her. His face tight, his lips held into a grim line. "I actually didn't say anything. I...I just moaned."

Amelia sat up in the bed, dislodging the bandage. It dropped down below her eye. "Moan? You were hurt?"

Lord Brinsley leaned over her and adjusted the bandage away from her eye. "I wasn't hurt. I moaned because of the enticing way you stood as striker."

He was so close she could feel the heat radiating off his body, and the touch of his fingers sent exhilarating pulsations throughout her body. "But I stand like everyone else."

"But you're not everyone else." His voice was gravelly as he tenderly tucked a tendril of hair behind her ear.

It took Amelia a moment to understand what Lord Brinsley meant. Her mouth made the shape long before the sound came out. "Oh."

"Yes, oh." His face softened and his lips curled into a smile as he watched her face flush scarlet.

With his lips curved upward into a tantalizing smile, he was the most enthralling man of her acquaintance.

"You could beat any men in cricket just by standing in the striker pose."

His words, and the way he said them, was turning her body into a burning inferno. She felt the heat slide down her throat, to her breasts, to her stomach…and beyond.

She wanted him to kiss her again—the same way, with his tongue deep in her mouth. She wanted to feel him pressed against her.

Neither of them moved or breathed—both frozen by the forceful attraction between them.

CHAPTER TEN

The next morning Amelia and Gwyneth stood in front of Helene's shop. Amelia hesitated to open the door, her reticule containing the two dolls stuffed with diamonds clutched to her chest. Her stomach fluttered and her head throbbed. She hadn't slept last night, kept awake by her tantalizing experience with Lord Brinsley and her nervousness about this visit. Could she actually lie to Helene, her close friend? With her tendency to turn beet-red when agitated, she wasn't exactly the best candidate for subterfuge.

Gwyneth lowered her voice to a whisper. "It's going to start to look suspicious if we continue to stand in front of the shop. We should go in." By the animation in her voice, Gwyneth wasn't worried about the deception, only excited by the chance for adventure.

"You'll follow my lead? You'll not make Helene uncomfortable?"

"My goodness, Amelia! You make me sound cruel."

Amelia sighed. "I'm sorry, but Helene is a friend, and she's been through so much. When you get enthusiastic, you sometimes forget everything else."

Gwyneth linked her arm in Amelia's and they entered the shop. "You're absolutely right. I'll try to curb my eagerness. And, like you, I really do value my friendship with Madame de Puis." Gwyneth then giggled. "She is the best modiste in London."

The strong scent of roses and cinnamon filled the fashionable space. Amelia loved Helene's élan for turning this very basic square room into a gorgeous cocoon of decadence and simplicity. With billowing white silk on the walls and drapes accented with gold, and the scent of roses, the shop was an enticing retreat for the crème of society's ladies.

At the tingling of bells above the door, Helene emerged from the back room. "Lady Gwyneth and Miss Amelia, you've come early?"

Amelia studied Helene's face, trying to reconcile whether her face was one of the French smugglers. She accepted that Helene had to buy from the smugglers to keep her business alive, but it would be a totally different proposition if Helene were herself a smuggler dealing in diamonds.

Gwyneth nudged Amelia with her elbow.

"I hope not too early, Helene. I wanted to show Lady Gwyneth the fabrics that have just arrived."

"Of course, you've brought the dolls?" As Helene stepped closer, she gasped aloud. "Miss Amelia, mon Dieu! What has happened to your face? Should you be out of bed?"

Amelia curled her lips into a smile of sorts. If she heard from one more person that she should remain in bed, she'd scream aloud. It had been hard enough to convince her father that the injury was nothing serious. Jack, her oldest brother, would arrive today and he'd be worse than her father in scolding and attempting to protect her. Like another forceful gentleman whom she'd been unable to put out of her mind since his tender care after the accident.

"I'm fine, Helene. I was hit with a cricket ball. The bruising looks a lot worse than the actual injury." She repeated her mantra. "I've never felt better."

Helene curtsied to Gwyneth. "Lady Gwyneth, the fabrics that Miss Amelia has chosen will look wonderful on you. You'll make a most beautiful bride."

"Thank you, Madame. I was so impatient to see the materials that I called on Miss Amelia early. I wanted to arrive before any other ladies."

Helene's smile didn't reach her eyes. "I understand...an impatient bride. Please be seated, and I'll have Elodie bring out the fabrics. May I get you champagne, tea, biscuits?"

They had planned to catch Helene off-guard. Amelia was to speak in a blasé manner. "Lady Gwyneth loves the dress design on the doll." Amelia's hand shook as she untied the knot in her reticule. She removed the dolls, wrapped in their silk and handed them to Helene.

"You'll look ravishing in that gown, and the veil is magnificent especially with the red accents, Lady Gwyneth," Helene said.

Amelia scrutinized the modiste's face for any hint of deception or artifice. Helene remained calm and composed. There were no obvious signs of anxiety at the appearance of the dolls. Amelia worried that Helene would notice the slight wrinkles in the fabric from Gus' drool.

"Thank you, Miss Amelia, for their prompt return. Lady Stamford has requested to view the newest dolls. She wasn't pleased at not having first priority."

Gwyneth's dark brows shot up in surprise.

Amelia ignored Gwyneth. It was preposterous to consider that Lady Stamford might be involved in smuggling. She was one of the ton's most respected ladies.

"I'll have Elodie take these dolls immediately to Lady Stamford," continued Helene.

Amelia nodded her understanding at Helene's urgency— Lady Stamford could be very demanding.

Helene unfolded each doll and inspected them carefully. Amelia's heart thundered up her chest, roaring into her ears. With Helene's attention to detail, she'd certainly notice that the doll's heads had been manipulated.

Amelia couldn't look at Gwyneth since she knew Gwyneth's expression mirrored their shared anxiety.

Satisfied with their appearance, Helene re-wrapped the dolls, and then opened the white silk drapes parted the show room from the work area. "Elodie?"

Elodie was one of the young French women recently hired to work in the shop. Helene employed many seamstresses throughout the city who worked on all the garments in their own rooms, but only two assistants worked on-site in the small shop.

A willowy girl with her dark hair pulled back in a heavy bun appeared at the curtain. "Yes, Madame."

Helene handed the girl the wrapped dolls. "Take these to Lady Stamford, and be quick about it."

"Yes, Madame." The young French girl kept her eyes downcast and her face averted, as she curtsied. Amelia saw nothing suspicious in the young woman's behavior since she was not more than eighteen years old and obviously nervous to be in front of ladies.

The young girl scurried out of the shop without looking back, the dolls clasped tightly to her breast.

Surely if Helene were involved, she would not have allowed the diamonds to leave her shop. Helene's composed expression gave no hint of guilt or worry.

Amelia hadn't wanted to let the diamonds out of her sight. How could they keep track of the diamonds now that they were leaving the shop?

As if their plan hadn't totally been changed by the fact that the dolls were gone, Gwyneth placed her hand on Helene's arm. "May I go to the back room to see where you work? Amelia has described the brilliant splendor of the fabrics, laces, and ribbons before they become your fabulous creations, and I simply must see them with my own eyes."

Helene's eyes narrowed, her voice severe. "My lady. It isn't proper."

"Proper?" Gwyneth's haughty tone, sounded like an outraged Aunt Euphemia. "I'm not allowed to see a room filled with fabrics and women sewing? Pray tell, why not?" Gwyneth had hoped to scrutinize the back room for clues to the mystery of the diamonds, but Amelia feared she was getting into her dramatic role a bit too much and would raise suspicions by her uncharacteristic curiosity.

Helene's face was enigmatic. The poor woman must be confounded by Gwyneth's sudden interest in pursuits much below her station. Amelia watched Gwyneth's black brows come together in a severe line so like her brother's. A determined Gwyneth wouldn't be easily thwarted.

Amelia needed to act fast. She swayed and reached for a chair. "I suddenly feel faint. Perhaps it was unwise to come out this morning."

Gwyneth grabbed her arm. "This is all my fault. I shouldn't have dragged you out of bed this morning. I'm going to take you straight home. Jenkins is waiting out front." Gwyneth's voice was so compassionate that Amelia wasn't sure if she caught on to the ploy or if she was truly concerned.

Amelia felt badly about acting a damsel in distress, but she must follow the smugglers to help her friend and her country. A fortune in diamonds could wreak havoc on England's safety. On the brink of rumored invasion by the French, the English were suspicious of the French already in the country. And if the ladies of the ton suspected that Helene's shop was the center of a smuggling ring, her business would never recover.

Helene's hazel eyes narrowed in question. "You do look pale."

Amelia had to swallow the retort she almost blurted out to defend her fair skin. "I am not…"

With a steadying arm around Amelia's shoulders, Gwyneth hustled her toward the door. "The sooner I get her home, the better."

Amelia turned back as Gwyneth guided her out the door. "Thank you, Helene. I'm sorry to have caused you worry. Lady Gwyneth and I'll return when I'm feeling better."

Gwyneth kept a firm grip on Amelia's arm and whispered. "Keep acting ill, in case we're being watched."

Amelia jerked her head up to look around. "Have you seen someone?"

"No, but from our experience at Christmas time, it is possible, and acting as if French spies were watching us makes our adventure much more exciting."

Amelia scoffed. Gwyneth was incorrigible, but also very sensible and capable—well beyond what her brother and Ash imagined.

Gwyneth maintained a brisk pace to the carriage. Jenkins hastened to put down the step and helped them ascend.

Amelia sat back against the cushioned seats and let out a deep sigh. "We've got to get to Lady Stamford right away before Elodie gets there."

"I assumed that was the plan behind your sudden fainting spell. You've never fainted in your life, have you?"

"No, only knocked un-conscious." Amelia touched her bruises, already turning purple and yellow, like Lord Brinsley's.

"Right. Sorry. But once we get to Lady Stamford, what then?"

"I've no idea." Amelia said.

They burst into laughter.

"We've got ten minutes to come up with something good." Gwyneth snickered.

"Do you know Lady Stamford well?" Amelia asked. "I can't believe she is part of a smuggling ring, but before the treachery at the Christmas party, I took everyone at face value. I didn't know your brother and Ash were spies."

"I don't believe Lady Stamford is smuggling diamonds. But as my aunt would say, assume nothing."

"Are Lady Stamford and your aunt close?"

"Lady Stamford is of an age with Aunt Euphemia. They debuted the same year. And, even though my aunt is quite eccentric and Lady Stamford is a formidable arbitrator in the ton on manners and fashion, they seem to be friends."

"Yes, Lady Stamford has been quite outspoken about some of my designs. She was positively apoplectic about my Greek toga dress."

They both tittered—remnants of their anxiety in going to Helene's shop. "What excuse are we going to use to call on Lady Stamford at this time of the morning? It must have something to do with your aunt since we'd have no other reason to make a call?"

"I could say Aunt Euphemia asked me to personally invite her to tea as her dearest friend."

"How will you explain the invitation to your aunt?"

"Aunt Euphemia won't mind if I invite her friend to tea. But I'd rather not tell Aunt Euphemia about the diamonds quite yet, or she'll use her serious imperious voice and counsel me to confide in Ash and Cord. And then I'd feel awful not obeying her."

"Since we know that Helene's not involved, maybe it's time to tell the gentlemen."

Gwyneth leaned toward Amelia. "We know that Helene's not involved, but will Cord or Ash accept our conclusion? And once they send someone to ask Helene questions, the ton will know within hours. And then the rumors will start."

A dull ache started in Amelia's chest and her headache pounded. Nothing about this business was straightforward. "You're right. We need to see if there is any connection with Lady Stamford, but I can't imagine that she could be involved with smugglers."

"Maybe it's one of her relatives taking the diamonds without Lady Stamford's knowledge? Or one of her servants?"

"Who are her relatives? Anyone suspicious?" Amelia's stomach coiled into knots with worry.

"She is widowed and has grown children." Gwyneth looked out the window. "We're almost there. We've got to settle on a plan."

"You can invite her for tea and then discuss the details of your wedding."

Gwyneth beamed. "Of course, and then I'll mention my wedding dress."

"Exactly. And I can bring up the dolls and my design. And then you can get very excited for her to see the doll."

"And then what?"

"A very good question with no answer. We'll improvise."

CHAPTER ELEVEN

Brinsley sat uncomfortably in a small chair, in the over-heated, over-decorated, gold and green parlor of Aunt Mabel's drawing room. He had arrived early, well ahead of his aunt's usual stream of visitors. He didn't want to shock the old biddies with his appearance. He shifted his weight again in the lady's chair. Most chairs considered fashionable were too small for him, but today his discomfort stemmed from a totally different reason. His aunt had fervently embraced his request—she'd make him respectable in society.

"You've made a wise choice in coming to me. It will be my greatest challenge to gain your entrée into society." Aunt Mabel's rheumy, but sharp eyes pored over his features. "But how am I to help you if you're still fighting and brawling?"

He shifted again, touching his hand to his eye. "This isn't what it seems."

"Tsk, tsk. You need to settle down with a good woman to stop your late night wanderings."

His aunt would be the first step of his plan to move forward along this path. He had a good woman picked out, but he couldn't mention that the woman was infatuated with her childhood friend. He planned to drive Amelia's juvenile fixation completely from her mind. He already knew she was partial to him, but until he could again move freely in society, he couldn't pursue her. Who would imagine, with his reputation that his interest was in an innocent red-haired cricket player?

His aunt continued on, requiring no input from him. He looked up; she'd asked him a question.

"It would make my task quite a bit easier, if Baron Lyon's daughter would make an appearance. You are aware of the latest rumors?"

"That I've fathered four children on her and left her abandoned and penniless in Scotland?"

"I'd only heard two children. I wonder if it was Emily Billingsworth who started the rumor of the four children. She took offense when I suggested that she consider a reducing diet."

He didn't care about the rumors, but Amelia, her father, and her brothers—they would care. He took a slow breath trying to ease the strain. Taking on society was more taxing than chasing French spies in Paris.

Aunt Mabel persisted. "Why won't Miss Lauren appear in society and put all the rumors to rest?"

"I believe she would find returning to society too stressful; it would cause her to relive all the memories. She's very happy living in Scotland."

His aunt puffed up her enormous chest. "Have you asked her? It would make my job a lot easier if she came forward and dispelled all the gossip."

He always found it hard to believe that this intimidating, hefty woman was related to his gentle, demure mother. He and his aunt took after the paternal side. His grandfather and his brothers on that side were built like oxen.

He shook his head. "I can't ask it of her. She has suffered enough."

His aunt pulled a handkerchief from her large bosom and patted at the tears in her eyes. "My sister would be very proud of the man you've become."

"Thank you, Aunt Mabel. I wish we still had my mother."

"As do I, my boy. In her honor, I won't rest until every hostess is vying for your attention. Fetch me my lap desk." She waved her hand to the corner of the salon. "It's sitting on my desk. I will start my campaign this very day." There would be no turning back now that Aunt Mabel had the marital gleam in her eye.

He walked to the desk as the salon door opened.

Hotchkiss, Aunt Mabel's aged butler, spoke in a voice of great consequence. "My lady, I'm sorry to interrupt. You have visitors."

"Visitors at this time of morning? Who would be calling at such an hour?"

Hotchkiss, like his mistress, knew everyone in society and their social importance. This individual must be quite significant. "It is Lady Gwyneth Beaumont and Miss Amelia Bonnington."

Every sinew in Brinsley's body tightened. Amelia here at Stamford mansion!

Aunt Mabel harrumphed. "Why are those two girls out and about at this ungodly hour? I sense intrigue here. Bring them in and bring another tray. My nephew, strapping boy that he is, needs his nourishment." She spoke with affection as she looked at the empty tray he had devoured.

Standing at his aunt's desk, Brinsley waited. Eagerness and dread skittered along his skin. He was a mix of conflicting emotions. He wasn't ready for Amelia to know the details of his past.

Shortly after the butler departed with the tray, Lady Gwyneth swept into the room with Amelia close behind.

"Lady Stamford, we're delighted to find you home this morning," Lady Gwyneth gushed in her exuberant voice.

Amelia's thick hair was pulled back on her neck, though tendrils of the fiery hair had escaped their constraints and framed her oval face beneath her bonnet. He wanted to tuck her wayward hair behind her tiny pink ear. He wanted to inhale her exotic female scent. He wanted a lot more, but one step at a time.

"My lady." Amelia and Lady Gwyneth both curtsied together, unaware of his presence in the corner.

"Ladies, what a pleasure to have two of society's favorite daughters visiting." His aunt seemed genuinely pleased.

"Please come and sit. Hotchkiss will return with a tray in a few moments."

He saw the conspiratorial smile exchanged between the two women. What game were they playing, and how did it involve his aunt? Both ladies still hadn't noticed him since they were focused on gaining entry into his aunt's salon.

"Are you acquainted with my nephew, Lord Brinsley?"

Both ladies turned so quickly, their surprise verily exploded from their faces. He needed all the control he could muster not to laugh aloud. Oh, they were definitely guilty of something.

He stepped away from the desk. "Lady Gwyneth. Miss Amelia." He bowed.

Lady Gwyneth recovered first. "Lord Brinsley, what a surprise to find you here." She smiled and moved closer, offering her hand.

Amelia stepped back and dropped her eyes, her long lashes closing down on her violet eyes, hiding any feelings.

Aunt Mabel remained in her ramrod posture on the settee. "Derrick, do tell how you've come to know such estimable ladies," she said in a voice that would not be denied.

He spoke to his aunt, but continued to stare at Amelia, waiting for her to look up at him. "Aunt Mabel, do allow the ladies to sit before you start your inquisition."

Amelia started. Her lashes lifted, treating him to the sight of her dazzling eyes. Her purple pelisse made her violet eyes darker, the color of the night sky, and her red hair brighter, more vibrant. Her direct look sent shock waves through his body. How could one woman's glance send his entire being into need and protectiveness at the same time?

Aware of his aunt's and Lady Gwyneth's keen interest, he couldn't look away, and Amelia seemed to be as helpless as he was.

Lady Gwyneth broke the uncomfortable tension. "Lady Stamford, your nephew is a good friend of my affianced,

Viscount Ashworth. Miss Amelia and I had the pleasure of his company at Lord Edworth's party."

"Mmm...hmm." His aunt didn't fool him for one minute. The way her eyes filled with speculation darting between him and Amelia. The old girl hadn't missed a thing. "Well now, this is a revelation."

Lady Gwyneth looked directly at his aunt as she removed her pelisse in the over-heated room. "It is time for your nephew to come back to society."

Aunt Mabel patted the seat next to her for Lady Gwyneth on the settee. "Please, Lady Gwyneth, come sit next to me. Miss Amelia, you sit next to my nephew." He didn't miss the way his aunt watched Amelia's porcelain skin take on a rosy color.

"My, my, what a beautiful blush. But what in heaven's name happened to your face?"

Oh, his aunt could be the devil.

"Aunt Mabel..." Brinsley tried to make his voice sound stern. He wouldn't allow his aunt to embarrass Amelia.

"Settle down, my boy. Miss Amelia doesn't need your protection, not from me. She's made of sterner stuff. Isn't that right?"

Amelia's lips curved into a subtle smile. "Yes, ma'am."

"My nephew, like all males, doesn't believe that women can take care of themselves." His aunt beamed at him.

Amelia's eyes sparkled. "Or believe a woman can play cricket proficiently." Amelia's voice and eyes were inviting and teasing as she smirked at him. And her affectionate regard softened the cold chill that had encased his heart for many, cold long years.

"This is turning into the most interesting morning." His aunt's voice was smug, filled with satisfaction as she kept her intense gaze on him.

Lady Gwyneth turned toward his aunt and spoke in her most cultured voice, "Lady Stamford, the reason we came by was to invite you to my ball next week—and it would be a perfect time for society to see that my brother and my fiancée both hold Brinsley in the highest regard."

Apparently Lady Gwyneth had decided independently of his aunt, to ease him into society. Both ladies were a force to be reckoned with, and he had no doubt in their ability to ease his way. The question remained, would their efforts influence Amelia?

"I just started a list of my acquaintances. I'll make sure each of them makes a point of speaking to him at your ball." His aunt added.

His aunt and Lady Gwyneth were talking as if he weren't present. He didn't mind, with Amelia sitting next to him, suddenly his world was in order.

He leaned closer to her, seeking the slightest contact with her. "Miss Amelia, what brings you and Lady Gwyneth out so early?" He had no idea how well Amelia knew his aunt. He hadn't been in society for four years, but he did know it was a very small and closed hierarchy.

Her eyes widened and her lips parted, as when he had kissed her. But this time it wasn't from arousal, but from surprise.

"We needed to see Madame de Puis early about Lady Gwyneth's wedding dress." She rushed the words as if they had been rehearsed. "And Aunt Euphemia wanted Lady Gwyneth to personally invite your aunt to tea."

He might have been shunned from society, but he still knew all the rules: ladies didn't call in person at this time of morning for an invitation. They sent engraved cards.

"Madame de Puis?" He was trained as a spy. He shouldn't have too much difficulty in discovering what the ladies were about.

Amelia averted her gaze, avoiding eye contact, as her hands twisted the cords in her reticule. She was easy to read as she purposefully avoided his question about the modiste. She'd never make it in his world of spies. Or maybe only he could read her so well.

"Lady Gwyneth, you've forgotten our reason for our visit, this morning," Amelia spoke in a tense tone he had never heard before.

"Of course. Lady Stamford, my aunt wants you to come to tea this week. Is there a day that is amenable to you?" Lady Gwyneth smoothed her dress as she spoke and avoided looking at Brinsley.

"How is dear Effie? I missed her at Emily's soiree. I'm surprised that she sent you out at such an early time."

"We had to visit Madame de Puis early to choose the fabric for my wedding gown. Since I was close by, I told Aunt Euphemia I'd deliver the message in person."

The way Lady Gwyneth's eyes darted back and forth, Brinsley was willing to bet his favorite riding boots that Aunt Euphemia knew nothing about this visit.

"Do you use Madame de Puis as your modiste, Lady Stamford?" Amelia asked in a sweet, innocent manner.

"Of course, she is the best. But I was put out and thought about taking my business elsewhere."

Lady Gwyneth startled. "Really, were you unhappy with Madame de Puis' work?"

"I've always found her work outstanding." Amelia leaned forward as if ready to defend.

"A bad fit or bad design?" Lady Gwyneth persisted.

"No, her gowns are wonderfully constructed. She lent the newly arrived fashion dolls to someone before me. I always am the first to see her dolls. She won't tell me who the customer was, but I'm sure Emily Billingsworth got in ahead of me for spite—all because of one remark about a reducing diet."

"How tiresome," Lady Gwyneth fanned her face with her hand in a very affected, most unusual way for the exuberant young woman. He had never spent time taking tea with ladies and was surprised by all their nuanced behavior. Teatime could be a training ground for spies, especially where women of society were involved.

"Have you seen the newest dolls?" Amelia asked intensely.

"Amelia is a wonderful designer, and it would be quite lovely if she could see the dolls," Lady Gwyneth chirped. "Have you received them yet?"

Amelia choked on her tea, coughing violently while covering her lips with her napkin.

"May I be of assistance, Miss Amelia?" He leaned over and touched her, his enormous hand spanned her entire back. The scent of honeysuckle wafted into his nostrils, driving his need to touch her, to breathe in her scent as he had on Christmas Eve.

She delicately patted her lips with her napkin. Her pale purple eyes were teary from the coughing spasm.

He wanted to pull her onto his lap and hold her. Seeing her in his aunt's sitting room, he wanted to belong to society only so he could be the only one next to her in any sitting room.

"Are you all right, Miss Amelia?" His aunt asked.

"Thank you, Lady Stamford. I'm fine."

His aunt caught his eye and winked at him. With their years of affection, she was sure to read all his feelings.

"Miss Amelia, now that you've recovered, would you like to see the dolls? Perhaps they will inspire your designs for my wedding ball." Lady Gwyneth stared at Amelia.

Brinsley leaned back in the narrow chair. He wanted to slap his knee in enjoyment. All the mystery was about fashion dolls. His aunt got first dibs on the dolls so Amelia and Lady Gwyneth wanted to see them. Such subterfuge around fashion wasn't worthy of these two. They both had handled themselves remarkably well during a harrowing experience at Edworth's party.

"I think this is my cue to leave." He stood. "Fashion dolls are not my forte."

"We didn't mean to run you off with our talk of fashion." Lady Gwyneth teased.

Amelia looked up at him as he stood. Her eyes and face were enigmatic and clouded with emotions impossible to read. She sat straighter in her chair. "I do remember you remarking that you found the pursuit of fashion loathsome."

What? Amelia remembered his cutting remarks from their first meeting. He had tried to be offensive, resisting the powerful pull she had on him even then. He liked that she was an artist, and obviously shared her talents with her friends.

"I do apologize, Miss Amelia, for any offensive comments I've made. I'm very ignorant of fashion." He looked at her, hoping to communicate that he found nothing lacking in her.

Whatever she saw in his eyes, made her retreat behind her long golden lashes. He watched her rounded breasts move in rapid breaths.

His aunt pulled the bell cord. Hotchkiss arrived so quickly that he must have been listening outside the door.

"Hotchkiss, have the fashion dolls arrived from Madame de Puis?"

"Yes, my lady. They just arrived."

"Please bring them to me."

Hotchkiss bowed his bald head and silently closed the door.

"Derrick, I'll expect you to escort me to Lady Gwyneth's ball. I'll host a dinner party with the newest marriageable debutantes and their mamas. Nothing gets acceptance into the ton, like an unwed, gentleman of means, even those with reputations."

Now, what was his aunt playing at? She was no fool. She had easily deduced how he felt about Amelia.

His aunt's lips were curved in a smug line as if she were Vice-Admiral Nelson and had outmaneuvered the French Navy. "Help me up. I shall walk you out."

What? His aunt never walked her guests out. It was unheard of and shocking. She must have something private to discuss. He hoped it wasn't about his obvious feelings for Amelia.

"Of course, aunt." He couldn't retreat now that he had engaged his aunt on a mission.

Lady Gwyneth sat up. "Lady Stamford, I'm afraid we're intruding. If you'd prefer for Miss Amelia and I to leave so you're able to finish your conversation with your nephew, we can come back another day."

"I'll only be a minute, and I look forward to discussing the newest fashion with our most revered fashion arbitrator, Miss Amelia."

His aunt respected Amelia's fashion taste. This was all new to Brinsley. Amelia was turning the pinkest of colors. He wanted to see that flush for another reason that he shouldn't be fantasizing about in his aunt's drawing room, but he couldn't stop when Amelia was so close.

Hotchkiss returned with the dolls.

"Please, Hotchkiss, give them to Miss Amelia."

"Thank you, Lady Stamford."

"But you must promise that you'll save all your conversation about the dresses until I get back."

"Of course, Lady Stamford." Amelia reassured, but something wasn't right about this business with the dolls. Amelia held the dolls nervously, not like someone who was anticipating the revelation of the latest fashion.

He bowed to the ladies. "Good day, Lady Gwyneth and Miss Amelia."

He walked to the settee to offer his arm to his aunt and they moved toward the door.

Once outside of the room, his aunt reached up and pinched his cheek as if he were a youngster. "Nice work, my boy."

"Whatever do you mean, Aunt Mabel?"

"Fiddlesticks, don't go all male on me. You know exactly what I'm talking about." She took his arm and moved toward the front door. "Those dark, brooding looks at Miss Amelia Bonnington. How fabulous. And her blushes…oh, my." She fanned her face vigorously with her thick hand. "Makes me want to swoon."

He had never in his life seen his aunt so worked up. His discomfort grew. His aunt was just like Edward Harcourt's dog. Once she had a stick between her teeth, she wouldn't desist from her fearsome meddling.

"Aunt Mabel…" He tried to interrupt her in his most stern voice.

She squeezed his arm affectionately. "I knew when the time came you'd make the right choice. Miss Amelia Bonnington is perfect. She is an amiable, well-respected young woman who is sensible."

"Aunt Mabel, the lady has been very clear…"

"You're the perfect match for her. Her father and brothers are all formidable men and Miss Amelia handles them all. You won't be able to intimidate her with your giant size and dark looks." His aunt clucked.

"Aunt Mabel, Miss Amelia isn't available." He wasn't sure how much to tell his aunt, but he didn't want her to harass Amelia. "She's interested in another gentleman."

"Everyone in society knows she and Kendal have been intended for each other since childhood. And I've always known that Kendal isn't the man for her. Trust me, if the lady were really interested in Kendal, he'd be a married man. Miss Amelia has had many suitors and she's used Kendal to keep them away. Kendal is young and impetuous and is in no way ready to settle down."

Hotchkiss stood, holding Brinsley's greatcoat. "Your coat, sir."

"Thank you, Hotchkiss." He put his arms into his coat as his aunt waited.

"Hotchkiss, go and see if the tray is ready for the ladies, please."

As Hotchkiss tottered down the hallway, his aunt whispered to him. "No need for Hotchkiss to know of my plans."

"What plans?"

"Keep up, Derrick. My dinner party. I plan to dangle a bit of competition in front of Miss Amelia's nose."

"But aunt, no families will allow their daughters near me."

"You'd be surprised how a rich, titled gentleman with plans for marriage can change popular opinion, and I plan to collect on a few favors. Expect to be a very sought-after gentleman at the ball. It will make Miss Amelia sit up and pay attention."

"But Aunt Mabel, I don't want Miss Amelia to…"

"Derrick, you do want Miss Amelia; that was as plain as the bruise on your face." She touched his cheek.

CHAPTER TWELVE

Amelia immediately stood when Hotchkiss departed. She couldn't draw air into her lungs and her hands trembled as she unwrapped the dolls. They were the same dolls, in the same incredibly beautiful garments. Nothing had been altered since she had seen them in the shop. She shook them close to her ear in an effort to hear them rattle. "I don't hear anything."

Gwyneth leaned close. "Are the diamonds gone?"

Amelia handed the doll with the wedding veil to Gwyneth. "You take this one's head off. I'll do the other. Quickly. We don't have much time."

Gwyneth took the doll and shook it. "Definitely lighter."

Gwyneth sat in the chair Lord Brinsley had vacated. "Can you believe Lady Stamford is Brinsley's aunt? I never made the connection because Brinsley hasn't been in society since I made my début."

Amelia didn't want to think of Lord Brinsley and the way his mere presence could make her stomach flip-flop and her skin skitter in awareness. She sat down and placed the doll on her lap to prevent the diamonds from falling on the floor. She twisted loose the head of the doll in the pale yellow dress. She felt guilty that she might damage such incredible perfection. "The diamonds are gone," she said breathlessly.

Gwyneth deftly turned the head of the bride doll. "Nothing in this one either. Who is our thief?"

Amelia couldn't stop her heart from racing as if she had just run the bases in a cricket game. "We can discuss this once we leave here. Put the head back on and get back in your chair. I think I hear someone."

Gwyneth giggled. "If Lady Stamford comes back, we can pretend the heads fell off."

Amelia tried to sound her sternest, but Gwyneth always made light of any situation. She reminded Amelia of Parker, her middle brother, who always was ready for adventure. "Stop laughing. Put your doll's head back on, now."

"You're worried now that you know Lady Stamford is related to Brinsley."

"Of all the most ridiculous ideas. Why would I care about Lord Brinsley's relatives?"

Gwyneth rolled her dark eyes.

Amelia whispered. "Lady Stamford can't be involved. She wouldn't have left us alone with the dolls if she knew there were diamonds."

Gwyneth whispered back, "And I can't imagine the guilty one is Hotchkiss. He's been in service with Lady Stamford since I first came here with my Aunt Euphemia as a little girl."

"That only leaves one person," Amelia said.

They said the name simultaneously. "Elodie."

Amelia shook her head in disbelief and stared at Gwyneth. "It must be Elodie. She's the only one besides us who has touched the dolls."

"We've got to figure out who is behind the smuggling and why."

"But with the diamonds gone, how are we going to prove there were diamonds?" Amelia stared at the doll as if it contained the answer to their problem. "We can wait for another shipment of dolls."

"But it could be months before Helene receives another shipment with the British blockade in the English Channel."

"We need to tell Cord and Ash about the diamonds. If the diamonds are being used by French spies, they must be informed," Amelia said.

"We could, but then Helene will come under suspicion. And then Ash wouldn't allow me to remain involved."

Amelia felt torn about the next action. She understood Gwyneth's frustration that Ash didn't acknowledge her ability, especially after she had saved his life. But Amelia needed to be sensible and decide what was best for both of her friends.

"Do you know anything of Elodie?" Gwyneth scrutinized Amelia's face, trying to read her intentions.

"No. She's been present in the shop for several months, but I only interact with Helene. She is the newest of Helene's helpers. She seems so young to be involved in clandestine activities.

"We need to find out more about her. Where she lives. When she came to England."

"I don't know. I guess I could ask Helene."

"We should follow Elodie from work to see where she goes, whom she meets."

Following Elodie sounded dangerous. Amelia needed to be the voice of reason. Gwyneth was impetuous and intent on proving her worth. After years of trying to prove herself to her brothers, Amelia understood. "I think we should report what we've uncovered to Ash and let him decide to pursue Elodie. I don't think we should get involved any farther."

Gwyneth pleaded with her dark brown eyes. "If you'd rather not go on, I can do this alone. I can ask Helene questions about Elodie. And Jenkins and I can follow Elodie when she leaves work. And once I've discovered her cohorts, I'll tell Ash."

This felt exactly like being involved in one of Parker's schemes. She never could say no to him. With Gwyneth's dark, pleading eyes, it appeared that she was unable to deny Gwyneth too. She certainly couldn't allow her to go alone.

Amelia raised her hands in the air for attention. "I will ask Helene about Elodie, then we'll decide whether we should follow her."

Gwyneth's lips curved into a knowing smirk. "You know we have to follow her. No matter what Helene tells you."

Amelia's mind spun. How could dress designing become so complicated?

CHAPTER THIRTEEN

Early the next morning, Amelia entered the modiste shop on her mission. Her plan was to question Helene about Elodie. She would've preferred to question the girl directly, but conversing with an unknown serving girl would raise too many suspicions.

Amelia was exhausted from another restless night. She wasn't sure if she was capable of deception when so tired. Struggling with the dilemma of whether to betray Gwyneth's trust and report the diamonds to Cord, as well as her inexplicable attraction to Lord Brinsley, had left her turning and twisting throughout the night. She didn't feel herself at all—nothing was familiar or constant in her world.

The sound of the tinkling bells and the heavy pungent smell of roses abraded her sluggish senses today. And Elodie, not Helene, was in the front of the shop.

The young girl with dark hair and very dark eyes curtsied. "My lady, Madame de Puis wasn't expecting you this early." She couldn't hide her wide eyes and the surprise in her voice. She dropped her head as if she realized she had spoken out of turn. "Madame de Puis isn't in the shop."

"It's quite all right. I had other errands in the neighborhood and I was anxious to drop off a few of my sketches for Lady Gwyneth's wedding trousseau." Amelia held up the rolls of paper in her hand. "You're Elodie, yes? You're new in the shop?" Amelia went into hyper-alert when Elodie's slight frame stiffened, her hands clenched next to her side.

"Yes, my lady. Madame de Puis has been very generous to me."

"Madame has told me what a skilled seamstress you are. I'd hoped that you might be able to help me with a few of my projects." Lying awake, Amelia had come up with this idea for how to feign interest in the young woman without arousing Helene's suspicions.

The young woman's face lit up. "Yes, mademoiselle...my lady. I'd like that a lot."

Nothing sinister or suspicious here that Amelia could detect.

"Do you have responsibilities for a family? Or would you be able to come to my house to work after you're finished with Madame."

Elodie shifted her weight, but kept her spine straight and her head lifted. "I take care of my two younger sisters since my mother died. Madame lets me take some of the sewing home and my sisters help."

Amelia inspected the young woman. Elodie was not more than eighteen, dressed in an ill-fitting frock of rough cotton, but delicate embroidery graced the neckline. The needlework was exquisite. The pattern on the round neckline was wildflowers in vibrant colors. "Did you do the lovely embroidery around your neckline?" Amelia asked.

Elodie reverently touched her neckline. "My sister Nathalie is very talented."

"Your sister is too young to work for Madame?"

"Yes, my lady." Elodie stared at her feet. "She is just twelve years old."

"And your other sister?"

"Jeanne is just eight."

"Well, if Madame approves, I could use your help. And like Madame, you can take the work home so you can attend to your sisters."

"Thank you, my lady." Her face, shining with enthusiasm, revealed her youthfulness. "That would be most helpful."

"Do you live close by to pick up and drop off your work?"

"I can pick up your work and return it when you need it, my lady. You do not need to worry."

Interesting. Elodie didn't want to share where she lived.

"It won't be a burden for you to travel when I need your work?"

"No, my lady. I can walk the miles."

"Wonderful. I'll speak to Madame de Puis the next time I'm in the shop. Can you give her these drawings?" Amelia handed the sketches to Elodie.

When Elodie reached, the sleeves of her dress raised up, revealing her forearms. Purple contusions marred both arms.

Elodie immediately pulled on her sleeves to cover the bruises. Amelia searched the young woman's face for any further signs of mistreatment. Elodie had no obvious marks. Amelia gritted her teeth in frustration and rage at the person who was abusing this young woman. Had Elodie become involved in something dangerous to support her two sisters?

Nothing would convince Amelia otherwise. Elodie was most likely an innocent victim in the diamond smuggling.

CHAPTER FOURTEEN

Amelia's childhood dream was coming true. Lord Michael Harcourt, Earl of Kendal, held her in his arms. His bright eyes, the high cheekbones, and the dimple in his chin were thoroughly familiar. She waited for the rush of emotions, the stirring of passion, the flitting of excitement. She felt none. Instead, she felt only comfort and fondness for her childhood companion.

"Amelia, what has happened?" Michael looked down as he twirled her in the cotillion. "You don't seem like the girl who tormented me my entire life."

She batted her eyes as she had done in the game they had played for so very long. "What do I seem like?"

"Different, especially in that get-up."

"Get-up?" She had spent her early years bantering with Michael. "This 'get-up' is the latest fashion."

"You know I don't recognize such things. Like Henrietta, I'm clueless when it comes to fashion."

"Yes, it does seem like the Harcourt family only appreciates patterns when they're related to codes."

"I like this new look. You look…chic…like a sophistiqué French woman." His eyes stared at the daring décolletage of her cerise gown.

He was saying words she had longed to hear for many years and she didn't care. He was finally recognizing her as a woman and all she wanted to do was laugh. "You've never seen me as more than a sister, never as a woman, have you?"

"A woman?" There was that roguish grin that used to make

her heart flutter and filled her dreams. "Well, I knew you weren't a man."

"High praise indeed. You never noticed my efforts to entice you to see beyond your childhood playmate."

"You must admit that some of your gowns were…interesting."

"Interesting? That is kinder than my brothers would've said. They've described them as atrocious."

Michael searched her face. His eyes and voice were serious, not the usual lighthearted teasing. "Amelia, are you saying that you've…"

Amelia squeezed his hand. "Michael, I fell in love with you when I was eleven years old."

"You did?" He genuinely looked shocked.

"Do you remember when my mother died giving birth to Drew?"

"Of course, it was terrible. Your mother was so lively and affectionate. She always made time for me."

"I was down at the river crying. I'd fled out of the house when my father told me. Not that I understood those feelings. I was only eleven, but I was devastated. You understood. You sat next to me and held my hand and told me that you would always be my friend. Then you made us both crowns of dandelions. We pretended you were a prince and I was a princess. You have been my real prince ever since that moment. You were my hero."

"I was quite a fanciful young boy back then. But I had no idea. You were Amelia, my sister's playmate."

"Yes, to my disappointment."

He pressed his hand to his chest. "You're very dear to me. I consider you a very close friend. I'm sorry if I've caused you pain."

There was the sensitive boy she'd loved. Underneath his roguish exterior, he was thoughtful and caring.

"You didn't cause any pain. You brought me stability in a moment when my world was falling apart. I confused that warmth and security for romantic love. You became my childhood fantasy. I envisioned that we would always share our own world, safe and free from pain."

"Well, in that revealing gown, I'd say you don't look at all like a childhood fantasy. You look like a grown man's fantasy." Then Michael stammered. "I don't mean my fantasy."

In that moment, Amelia realized, like all childhood fancies, hers had come to an end. Another man, a man who looked at her with burning intensity, now filled her dreams and made her world feel safe.

Michael swung her in a full circle. She threw her head back and laughed. She had never felt freer in her life.

Brinsley watched Amelia and the Earl of Kendal dancing together. Kendal held her close, too close. They stared into each other's eyes. Their mutual feelings clearly showed on their faces.

Amelia's shining face, filled with love for Kendal delivered a sucker punch to his gut. What a fool he had been. Kendal was as much in love with Amelia as she was with him. His head pounded, and he felt sick—heart sick.

Despite his pain, he couldn't look away from the enraptured couple. Kendal now pressed his hand against his heart. Could the jagged pain in his gut get any worse? He never stood a chance of winning Amelia's heart.

Brinsley could hear the nearby matrons sigh.

Kendal devoured her with his eyes. Possessiveness gripped his body. He wanted to hurt someone. He needed to get the hell away from the ballroom before he did some damage. But he was committed to dance with several more young women.

Kendal swung Amelia into a turn; she threw her head back and laughed. His aunt had already said that all of society merely awaited the engagement announcement of the perfect couple. His decision to re-enter society was a joke, a terrible bitter joke. This was absolute torture to watch Amelia, ravishing in a red gown that hugged her willowy curves, relish being in the arms of the man she loved. She was the reason he had endured the tedious dinner with his aunt and several eligible debutantes. He couldn't leave this ball and disappoint his aunt, the only person in his life who actually cared about him.

"The dancing looks like great fun."

He looked down at the buxom, blond debutante with calculating, blue eyes. He had totally forgotten her. He felt the heat grow under his collar. He was embarrassed to be caught in such an exposed moment.

He forced a smile at her. It wasn't her fault that they both were forced to play this charade. He was old and jaded at the ripe age of thirty-one. He couldn't possibly consider marriage to any of these young women who considered themselves sophisticated when actually they were quite innocent and oh so young. They were excited to play at this new game, a game he found utterly boring.

"Your time will come." He meant it, but he wouldn't be taking part.

His aunt approached with another dowager. His aunt was making sure he was paraded in front of all the dowagers of influence. This woman was dressed in a bright green outfit. She wore an outrageous turban that looked to be filled with birds. He'd never seen anything like this monstrosity. He marveled that she could keep the eyesore balanced on her head.

"Effie, I want you to meet my nephew." His aunt had her arm linked with the other woman. It was obvious that Aunt Mabel felt affection for this odd duck.

He found it difficult to look away from the birds perched on the dowager's turban.

"Derrick, this is Lady Beaumont, the Earl of Rathbourne's aunt."

Lady Gwyneth had mentioned the aunt, but he had never met her in his meetings at Rathbourne house.

He bowed. "Lady Beaumont. It's a pleasure. And may I introduce you to Lady Edith."

The girl at his elbow curtsied.

Lady Beaumont smiled at the young debutante. "Your first ball, I've been told, Lady Edith."

"Yes, my lady."

"Is your dance card full for tonight?" Lady Beaumont asked.

"Yes, I haven't missed one dance except for the cotillion. Lord Brinsley thought it would be a good idea for me to rest."

His aunt took Lady Edith's arm. "Let me take you back to your mother since I see the next gentleman is waiting for you."

Oh his aunt was doing her usual impression of Major-General Wellington. What it had to do with Lady Beaumont he couldn't surmise.

"I'm very happy to finally make your acquaintance. Gwyneth can't stop speaking of you and how helpful you've been to her," Lady Beaumont said.

He looked up sharply. The wrinkles around her bright eyes were intense, and she didn't miss his surprise.

Was she actually privy to her nephew's work? He had no idea, but he wasn't in a position to discuss assassination plots against the Prince of Wales.

"I was pleased to be of service, my lady."

"Yes, your service has been duly noted. I'm glad to see you back in society. This is what your mother would've wished for you."

"You knew my mother?" He couldn't hide his incredulity. He never had an opportunity to speak with anyone about his mother except his Aunt Mabel, and their conversations were filled with regret and their shared loss.

"I knew Lucy very well. Mabel and I came out the same year and became fast friends. Your mother debuted after us, but she was the belle of her year. Unlike Mabel, poor woman, who took after her father, your mother was feminine and petite, and the most congenial, sweetest woman I had ever met."

The thought of his mother, young and carefree, started a hurt in his chest rolling to a painful lump in his throat.

Lady Beaumont examined his face carefully. He couldn't surmise what she might be searching for, but whatever she saw pleased her. "It was a shame that she was forced to marry your father. He was known as a brute even as a young man."

The rage he harbored for so many years riddled his body. If the old man weren't dead, he'd still find pleasure in ripping him apart. As a child, he and his mother had been helpless to stop the cruelty.

"Not many people knew, but I know your mother suffered at his hand. And I suspect the reason you concocted the ruse to escape with your brother's fiancée was to prevent what you couldn't stop in your childhood."

He couldn't breathe. His lungs moved, but no air passed into them. Crushing pain gripped his chest. No one knew about his past except his Aunt Mabel. Had his aunt confided in this woman?

Lady Beaumont's voice was quiet and serious. "I'm glad you saved Baron Lyon's daughter from a fate your mother was forced to endure."

He had intervened to prevent his brother, who looked and behaved like his father, from harming a dear childhood friend. Gentle Lauren would never have survived a marriage to his brother. He never regretted his actions.

The old woman patted him on the arm. "I want you to know—now that you're spending time with Gwyneth and Cord, I'd love to tell you stories about your mother that Mabel might not remember. I hope you'll join us for tea soon."

He hadn't cried since his mother died, but he felt the tears burning behind his eyes. "I'd be honored to join you, Lady Beaumont."

"Forget the Lady Beaumont. You must call me Aunt Euphemia as all the family does."

The festering wound of not belonging, of not having a loving family, felt exposed. With his head down to hide the emotions that were churning in his heart, he didn't see Amelia approaching.

"Aunt Euphemia." Amelia curtsied. "As always, you look your unique self."

Aunt Euphemia chortled. "Don't try to hoodwink me, Amelia dear. I know full well you'd love to redo my wardrobe."

Aunt Euphemia turned toward Brinsley. "Amelia is a very talented artist and is consulted by all ladies of fashion. Did you know about her creative abilities?"

"I did know. Miss Amelia is a woman of many talents." He tried, but he couldn't stop staring at her. Her red hair was down and partially wound into a plait that hung over her shoulder. He wanted to unravel the flaming mane and...

Aunt Euphemia looked at him and then back at Amelia, her keen eyes flitting back and forth between them. Amelia's eyes were sparkling—she'd be every man's fantasy with her creamy white skin revealed, her luscious pink lips, and her air of joie de vivre.

Aunt Euphemia patted his arm. "I hope you'll soon come to Rathbourne house for tea. I'd love to reminisce about earlier, happy times."

"Thank you, Lady Beaumont, I mean, Aunt Euphemia. I'd like that." He bowed his head.

"Oh, look, Emily Billingsworth has arrived." Aunt Euphemia's eyes flickered with mischief. "Can you believe the outrageous color of her dress? At her age, she really should choose more somber colors." Aunt Euphemia chortled. "I must go and greet her."

He watched Aunt Euphemia march away. He didn't look at Amelia who stood before him. He didn't want her to see the hurt that was devouring him by having her so close but oh so unobtainable. Her face and eyes remained shining and open with excitement, all because of Kendal.

He felt her scrutiny, but he refused to suffer more by seeing the happiness shimmering in her eyes. Not with the freshly open wounds of his past as well as his desperate need for her seething inside him, he wasn't capable of engaging in the social niceties with her.

"Derrick, what is it? What's wrong?"

He jerked his head up. At this moment, she decided to call him by his first name.

Her eyes had softened and her flushed lips, the color of her dress, were parted in concern.

Her open and caring look for him was like acid burning his skin. He had to get away from this much pain. Why was she here tormenting him? Why didn't she go back to Kendal? He had to separate himself from her. He'd be damned before he let her know how he felt. He bowed formally. "Nothing is wrong. I'm enjoying my return to society."

"You look upset. Did someone offend you? Slight you?"

This would almost be funny if it weren't so agonizingly painful. That she had no clue how he felt about her and thought he'd be upset by any slight from such blatant hypocrites. Should he go for honesty? How would his little Miss Prissy fare with the brutal truth that he burned for her? He wanted things from her that she had no experience or imagination to consider.

"Congratulations are in order. I wish you the best." He gave her a curt nod. "If you'll excuse me, I'm to dance next with Lady Rowley."

He walked away from her, just as he had walked away from his father and brother. He had done it before; he could do it again. He didn't need anyone. He was well-experienced in shutting himself off. He'd been doing it his entire life.

CHAPTER FIFTEEN

Stunned by his abrupt manner, and his obvious rejection, Amelia stood in shock and watched Derrick walk away. What a striking figure he cut in his formal clothes. In black and white, he looked formidable and aloof, and more appealing. But she knew his soft and caring side, and she would've chosen a waistcoat with spring colors of gold or green for him.

All the young debutantes and married women watched him make his way with his forceful stride across the crowded ballroom.

Her feelings were reeling. Why had he treated her so cold and distant? She had gotten use to his intense stares and his enticing smiles. He seemed to be both hurt and angry. Aunt Euphemia had referred to better times.

Whatever had distressed him, he showed no inclination to talk to her. And what had he said to her after Aunt Euphemia left? "Congratulations…" Awareness dawned. He had witnessed Michael and her together and concluded that she still cared about Michael. Was that the reason for his hasty departure and his rejection of her?

She needed to talk with him, explain that she was finally clear about her feelings for Michael. But how could she explain to the foolish man when he wasn't going to listen? She had to find a way to make him listen. She also needed his help in rescuing Elodie.

She'd wait for a break after his dance with Lady Rowley. Why had his aunt arranged for him to dance with the flirtatious widow?

Derrick didn't seem to mind the crude cut of the dress or the way her wobbly breasts jiggled. In fact, his eyes hadn't left Lady Rowley's very voluptuous bosom the entire time they danced.

Her face burned to watch his obvious attraction and the woman's blatant flirtation. The lady had feigned ignorance of the turn in the dance, allowing herself to bump against him, so he had to catch her from stumbling, affording him a perfect view down her dress. Derrick smiled at the lady in appreciation. Jealousy and anger formed a molten mix of hurt.

Just then Derrick looked up at her, as if he knew she was blazing with jealousy. He gave her a cold smile, filled with a grim satisfaction. The look scalded her. Why was he angry with her? He was the one flaunting himself with Lady Rowley.

"What's got you seeing red?" Her middle brother, Parker, had come up behind her. "Your face is that unbecoming blush. Someone's got you riled."

"Go away." She hissed.

"Not when you're so much fun to torment." Parker stood next to her. With his blond hair and violet eyes, her younger brother was absolutely handsome. He had the same roguish appeal as Michael Harcourt—devastating to women's hearts.

"Who are you watching?"

"Did I not already ask you to go away?"

"Not when you're standing by yourself positively fuming."

"Where's Jack?"

"Not going to work. Oh, my…did you just see where Lady Rowley put her hands on that lucky fellow. Who is that gentleman so willing to be attacked by the barracuda?"

"The barracuda?" Amelia finally tore her eyes away from Derrick making a fool of himself.

"Lady Rowley. She's insatiable," Parker said.

"What? How do you know such things?"

"I'm male and I'm twenty-six years old. I know such things. Besides, Jack told me."

"Jack?" Her voice got shrill. "Are you telling me that Jack and…?"

"Don't go all prudish on me. Jack was probably only repeating rumors."

The idea of Jack and now Derrick with that woman—Amelia shook her head. Was there any hope for the male species? Well, if Derrick wanted to make a fool of himself on his first night back in society, she wasn't about to stop him. But she had seen the hurt on his face before he went off to pursue the ever so ripe Lady Rowley.

She turned to her brother. "Parker, I'm glad you're in town. I need your escort tomorrow evening."

"Escort? Do I have to? Please say it isn't a music concert."

"No, this might get dangerous. We're going to follow a young woman who is involved in a smuggling ring. You might get to knock a few heads together."

"This sounds like my kind of entertainment. Who is this young woman? And does Jack know what you're up to?"

"No, and you're not going to tell him. Must I remind you about your little…disagreement at the *Rooster Tail* tavern?"

Her brother might be blond, but he shared the same volatile skin color. Now it was her turn to enjoy the blush moving up his neck into his cheeks. "You promised not to rat on me."

"I won't. But not a word to Jack or anyone about tomorrow night."

With Parker's help, she no longer needed, or wanted, Derrick's help.

CHAPTER SIXTEEN

Brinsley sat in his regular spot, watching the front door of *Ship's Aground* tavern. He leaned against the damp wall of the tavern, trying to escape Bev's wandering hands. After last night's episode with Lady Rowley, he wasn't in the mood for pushy women and their games. The only hands he wanted on him were artistic, slender, and porcelain pale. Convinced that was never going to happen, he wanted nothing to do with women at all.

His muscles tightened, but not for what Bev was offering. He was ready for a violent and bloody distraction. He should've laughed at the irony of his situation, but he could find no humor when one woman had him reeling.

"Bev, you want another drink?" he asked.

"You know what I want." Bev ran her tongue along her lower painted lip.

"I've got business here in the tavern." He was ready to have this operation finished. Tonight should be the end of this masquerade. Based on reliable intel, the French planned to make their buy.

Instead of Ash, he had Talley as backup. New to the tavern, Talley, with his blond hair and devilish grin was getting a lot of notice by the "waitresses" who flitted between the tables of men, offering their wares.

"Tell me again what you saw." He struggled to sound patient.

Bev sucked in a big breath, making her breasts partially slide from their mooring in the flimsy dress. "Like I said, he came in last week, dressed like usual—a woolen scarf wrapped around his face, a hat pulled down low so you couldn't see nothing but his eyes. He sat in the corner by himself. Rough men and gents come and talk to him, one by one. It's as if he be holding court."

"And what happened when you approached?"

She leaned toward him, her breasts pressing against his arm. "I knew you might be interested in what he was doing so I sashayed over there, nice and pretty, just to say hello. But Harry pulled me away. He told me it wasn't for the likes of me."

"You think Harry is involved?" he asked.

"No, Harry keeps his nose down. He was warning me off since it was dangerous."

"Why would Harry do that?"

"Harry looks out for me—steers me away from the bad blokes."

"I'm glad Harry is looking out for you. Bad things can happen at a place like this."

"I can tell the difference. I knew you were a good guy right from the first." Bev smiled broadly, showing her one missing tooth.

The door opened and he went on the alert. Instead of the English mole he waited for, a young girl with a thin shawl wrapped around her scrawny shoulders—not enough to keep her warm—walked through the door. She searched the room. *Ship's Aground* was no place for such a young girl. She approached a lone man leaning on his table, obviously deep in his cups.

The older man wasn't pleased to see her by the scowl on his face. He had witnessed many tragic scenes just like the one that transpired in front of him. The girl sat down and spoke quietly to the man. It was pitiful to watch—he didn't need to hear her words, her dark eyes pleading for her father to come home said it all.

The man grabbed her by her arm. She winced in pain, but didn't try to pull away. Brinsley shifted his weight in his chair, getting ready to intervene. He knew he wasn't supposed to break cover, but if the man didn't release her arm, he'd have to act.

Keeping part of his attention on the girl, he turned to the sound of the tavern door opening once more. Two dandies in riding breeches, their top hats pulled over their foreheads as if to hide their identities, stood at the door. Their obvious, expensive clothes and their discomfort had caused the whole room to go silent. Every face turned to watch their entrance. They couldn't be the French buyers since they showed no hesitation in making a conspicuous entrance. Were they a distraction? He sat up and scanned the room to make sure all appeared status quo.

The gentlemen moved further into the tavern and everyone returned to their drinks. The taller of the two had blond hair and looked vaguely familiar. Brinsley tried to remember where he had seen him and what his appearance might mean to tonight's mission. As the two walked toward an empty table, Brinsley inspected the shorter man walking behind.

The blood rushed through his ears, making him light-headed. For one of the few times in his life, Brinsley suffered a complete and total loss of awareness. Dressed as a man, but looking more like a boy, Amelia had entered this black hole of thugs and spies.

He'd recognize that retroussé nose and violet eyes through any disguise. The other man must be her brother, the one she had been with last night while he danced with Lady Rowley.

He must have tightened his grip on Bev's arm since she leaned against him, misreading his furious reaction for something more primal.

Amelia set off frenzied and frantic reactions. She robbed him of his natural demeanor—calm control and focused attention.

This could only be the worst kind of coincidence, her being here when the French spies were expected to buy the secret. But what had brought her here, and why tonight?

His mind was whirling with possible implications. His mission had just done a complete turn-about. His mind raced through several scenarios, but none with a happy ending. How could he keep Amelia safe if things got hazardous? He and Talley had to capture the Navy's traitor, and the French spies.

They expected the French spies would leave first. Talley and his men would follow and capture the French red-handed with the Navy's plans in hand. It would be up to him to grab the traitor. Additional agents were seated around the tavern if he needed assistance. He couldn't allow Amelia to get caught in the crossfire, but how could he possibly remove her from the tavern without totally blowing his mission.

Amelia settled into a chair as Harry moved over to serve the two esteemed gentleman. She searched the room then stopped her perusal when she saw the young girl. Amelia leaned forward to better inspect the man with whom the girl spoke fervently. Amelia obviously had some connection with the girl. Did she have any idea the danger she might encounter? The men who frequented the tavern were ruthless criminals and would stop at nothing.

He watched her, waiting for the moment she recognized him. Her eyes widened, and he imagined he could feel her accelerated breathing as her lips parted in recognition.

He stared at her, fully resolved not to hide his seething emotions. She looked at Bev who was running her hand down his arm at that moment. He could see the way she jolted back in revulsion. Then those thick lashes went down, shutting in any reaction. Totally dismissing him, she turned and spoke to her brother. The best situation was for her to think of him as a wastrel rather than realize he was on a mission.

Her brother slowly looked around the room as if doing his own reconnaissance. What the hell did that young pup think he could do? He wanted to mangle the young fool for bringing his sister into danger, but knowing Amelia's strong will, he guessed her brother had no choice.

"Do you know those gentleman?" Bev asked.

Unfortunately, he had betrayed his connection to Amelia and her brother. Observant Bev was no fool. "I do know them. Young bucks out for a little fun on the seamier side of town."

"With money to waste." Bev puckered her mouth in anticipation.

He didn't want to call attention to Amelia and her brother. "Can you get them out of here if any trouble starts to happen? They'll just get in the way. I know their mother and don't want her to be upset by the silly fools getting hurt. I'll make it worth your time."

"I can take them out the back way."

He had no way of knowing if Bev could be trusted, but what choice did he have now that Amelia had sashayed into the middle of his operation. He dug for his bag of coins in the lining of his jacket. "Go over to their table and play it up with the blond man. Make it appear like you're looking for a little fun with them. And then take them out the back way and tell them I said to get the hell away from here."

"But I'll come back once they're gone. You did promise me a bit of fun for all my effort."

"Of course, once my business is settled." He gave her a look that she could not misinterpret, a woman of her experience.

She leaned down and kissed him on the lips. "You better not change your mind."

Playing along, he swatted Bev on her full, round ass when she turned. She cackled loudly, causing Amelia to turn.

Amelia looked straight at him. He wanted to shake her and shout at her for coming into danger, but at the same time he wanted to hold her and protect her. He took a big gulp of his ale and looked away from her close inspection. He needed no extra attention focused on either of them.

Amelia's eyes widened in shock when Bev sauntered to their table. His little prude was turning red from Bev's overtures. Brinsley would have preferred to protect her from the seediness, but she was the one who chose to come to a dockside tavern in the worst part of London. Unbelievable. She might as well go into treacherous St. Giles looking for adventure.

Bev bent over the table, flirting with Amelia's brother, giving him an eyeful of her breasts. He stood and offered Bev a chair.

Amelia's attention was on the young girl and her interaction with the man Brinsley surmised was her father. He sure hoped to hell the old bastard wasn't the young girl's lover or pimp, and that Amelia had come here with some notion of saving her in some manner.

Tonight's mission had gotten complicated in ways he hadn't considered. Now the potential for things to go sideways was tremendous. Because of Amelia's innocent presence, he couldn't find the calm he usually had when about to close on a quarry. He needed to settle his racing heart and figure out how he could keep her and her brother safe.

The door opened again, and of all the luck, tonight his suspect had arrived. Wrapped in the scarf and hat, the thin man confidently made his way into the tavern. This was no dockworker trying to sell the secrets to make money for his family, shooting down one of the theories that had been bandied about.

Brinsley sat back against the wall, trying to act nonchalant as he surreptitiously checked to make sure all his men were in place.

Talley too had noted the suspect's arrival. He had removed one of the waitresses from his lap, teasing her and sending her for more drinks. The din in the room grew louder and more raucous.

Harry greeted the man and led him to the corner table. Harry kept his head lowered in a subservient manner as if he recognized the man's treachery.

Brinsley's attention was drawn to the sound of a chair scraping briefly on the floor. The young girl's father stood; the girl grabbed him by the arm, begging him. He slapped her across the face, knocking her to the floor, sobbing.

Amelia gasped and jumped from her chair at the violence. Her hat fell off revealing her bright red hair twisted in a braid that cascaded down her shoulders and back.

One of the brawny dockworkers shouted, "He's no bloke. It's a woman in breeches." All the men jumped to their feet, some gawking, some pushed close, and some needing much more. One of the men fell into a waitress, who landed in the lap of a disgruntled drunk, making him drop his drink. In the bedlam, the first punch was thrown and pandemonium broke out.

Realizing her peril, Amelia tried to stuff her hair back into her hat, but got caught in the men shoving toward her. She was knocked to the ground.

As punches, glasses and even bottles were thrown, the father made his way through the wild fracas toward their suspect in the corner.

Brinsley, keeping the men in his sight, pushed his way toward Amelia and her brother. Her brother was smiling as he punched the man who had knocked Amelia down. Her brother pulled her up to stand and then had to punch another man who came at his side. Young though he was, he handled himself well in a fight.

Brinsley had no time for the nonsense. He picked up one guy and threw him against another brute to get to Amelia.

Keeping his attention on the man in the corner, Brinsley shoved his way through the belligerent crowd. The girl's father and the man with the scarf were in conversation at the table. The man didn't seem fazed by the violence.

Talley gave him a nod across the mayhem, signaling they would stick with the plan for Talley to apprehend the father once he finished his business. Was the father the French spy buying the secrets?

Brinsley had to knock out two brutes before reaching Amelia who was held in the arms of a huge thug who was trying to take her hat. She shouted in outrage and kicked the man in the shin. The man laughed and bent to kiss her.

Rage boiled beneath Brinsley's skin. He picked up the barbarian and threw him across the table.

Amelia stared up at him. "Derrick?" Her pupils were dilated and her hair hung loose around her shoulders.

He snatched up her hat and handed it to her. "Say nothing. And put the damn hat back on."

Bev was pulling on Amelia's brother's arm.

Brinsley yelled at Bev, "Get them out of here."

Bev nodded and said something to the brother. He looked shocked by whatever she said.

Amelia's face was flushed from exertion as she tucked her hair into her hat. Her cravat had come undone, and he could see her pale skin. "Bev will take you out the back way to your carriage."

He shoved Amelia's brother. "Get your sister away from here."

"Yes, sir."

He watched the brother put his arm around her shoulders as they made their way through the crowd to the back door.

Now that Amelia and her brother were safe, he could focus on his mission. The man in the corner leaned against the wall, his body twisted into an unnatural posture. His hat was gone, his dark hair hung over his blank eyes.

Brinsley searched the crowd for Talley. He was gone, as was the girl and her father.

Brinsley fought his way to the table where the suspect remained motionless. With the chaotic fighting, no one had noticed the man's grim condition. The man's breaths came in erratic wheezes that shook his chest. Brinsley recognized the movement for what it was—death rattle.

Brinsley opened the man's waistcoat; his shirt was soaked in blood. Brinsley struggled to feel for his weak pulse.

Leaning over the man, Brinsley shouted to be heard over the chaos. "Who are you? Who do you work for?"

The dying man's answer was unintelligible in French.

Brinsley leaned closer to the man's wan face. "Who do you work for?"

The man fought for a breath.

Brinsley repeated, "Who do you work for?"

"*Elle,*" The man gasped.

Brinsley grabbed the man's shirt. "*Elle* or is it *il*? Do you work for a woman or a man?"

He mumbled another word, then his head dropped on his chest. Dead.

CHAPTER SEVENTEEN

Amelia sat alone on the settee facing Cord and Derrick. Gwyneth had confessed all of their activities to Ash, who then reported every detail to the two very grim gentlemen. After her part in the previous evening's disturbance, Amelia felt like a schoolgirl summoned to the head mistress' office.

Cord had requested her appearance in his official capacity, something not to be taken lightly—he wasn't acting as her childhood friend's husband. At least Cord didn't withdraw behind his desk as the fierce Director of Intelligence. She couldn't be totally intimidated by Cord since she only knew him as Henrietta's considerate and caring husband.

If anyone was trying to intimidate her it was Derrick. He exuded barely suppressed feelings of anger and resentment. And although Derrick never looked directly at her, she knew he was in a dangerous mood. His insolent slouch was gone. Instead his feet were solidly planted on the ground, his oversized, tense body ready to spring out of the leather chair.

His veiled hostility was a direct result of her disrupting his undercover operation. She didn't realize she had stumbled into a mission until she spotted both Derrick and Talley at the tavern. Talley was an agent who helped them capture the French villains at the Elwood party. She couldn't fault Derrick's reaction. But she hadn't known that Elodie was possibly involved in treason.

Derrick's eyes were focused straight ahead over her shoulder. All emotion shut off and locked down.

She refused to be daunted by Derrick's fuming mood. If he had been willing to talk with her at the ball, they wouldn't be in this predicament. She looked directly at Cord and spoke in a clear, precise tone. "I had planned to tell Lord Brinsley at the ball about the connection to Elodie, but he refused to talk to me."

Derrick startled and bolted upright. "What?"

"If you remember, I approached you at the ball, but you left abruptly to dance with Lady Rowley."

"You said nothing. How was I to guess you planned to endanger yourself and my operation?"

"Of all the most ridiculous responses. I didn't plan to endanger myself or your mission. How can anyone plan to endanger themselves?"

"Anyone with any sense knows the docks are treacherous. I would've made time to talk with you if I knew you were involved with a smuggling ring."

Amelia felt the sting of his cold, sharp words deep in her chest. He didn't care about her. Their kiss had meant nothing to him. He had been flirting with her as he did with every woman, as evidenced by his dalliance with Lady Rowley, and then there was that hussy at the tavern. With the hurt curling around her heart, she dredged up her most haughty tone. "How very generous of you."

She couldn't let her wounded feelings interfere with the more important work at hand, cracking the smuggling ring. "You're right. I should've told you, but you were so abrupt." She shook her head. She didn't want to confess that her pride had been hurt and she reacted with an impulsive plan.

"Instead you decided to embark on a ridiculous plan that took you to the most dangerous area of London? Do you know what could've happened to you?" Derrick's voice grew louder and harsher. His face was turning a purplish red, as if he might combust.

"I didn't know we were going to the docks until we followed her."

Derrick jumped to his feet. "Of all the asinine…When you

saw where she was headed you should have turned around and gone home like any sensible person would do."

She gasped.

Cord interrupted Derrick's tirade. "This is irrelevant now. We need to move forward. Tell us everything you know about the French girl."

Derrick sat back down, but continued staring at her, quietly fuming.

"When Gwyneth and I realized that Elodie was the link between the dolls and the diamonds, I went to Madame de Puis' shop to question her."

Derrick interrupted. "You should've told us right away when you discovered the diamonds."

Amelia twisted the handkerchief in her lap. How could she explain how protective she felt for Helene? And after discovering Elodie's bruises, she couldn't betray her either, not until she understood the abusive situation. "I fully intended to tell everyone once I knew that Helene wasn't involved."

Cord's formal manner softened and he nodded. "Gwyneth explained how you wanted to protect your friend."

Hearing Derrick's grunt of annoyance, Amelia continued. "Helene's business is based on her reputation, and you both know how fickle the ton can be. If there were rumors…"

"Yes, I understand." Cord encouraged her with his calm and accepting manner. "Once you realized your friend wasn't involved and that Elodie was the courier for the diamonds, what did you do?"

"Elodie works for Helene, so the risk for Helene is still present. Before I told you and Helene about Elodie's involvement, I wanted proof, so I pursued the young girl myself. I couldn't have you men all over Helene's shop, questioning her. The talk would have been brutal."

Derrick shifted in his chair, his impatience pulsating throughout the room.

"Gwyneth told me that you had wanted to communicate all at this point, but she encouraged you to continue your own investigation. Gwyneth wanted to impress both Ash and me with her skills."

Derrick turned quickly to look at Cord at the revelation that Amelia obviously wasn't as reckless as he believed. She didn't care at this point if she gained the brute's good opinion, but she was grateful to Gwyneth for her honesty. Amelia would never have exposed her friend's part in the misadventure.

"Gwyneth is highly capable, and I don't think you or Ash should dismiss her talents."

Derrick rolled his eyes.

All her fear and hurt rolled into a mass of explosive emotions. "Don't you dare roll your eyes at me, Derrick Jeremy Brinsley. Gwyneth and I aren't some flighty young girls looking for adventure. We proved our abilities at the house party, searching for clues when Ash was unconscious."

Cord's blue eyes lightened in amusement. She didn't find it funny when Derrick was behaving like a pig-headed bully. She was finding it difficult to remain patient as he exuded disdain and censure.

Ignoring her emotional outburst, Cord spoke in an unruffled voice "I'm very aware of both your and Gwyneth's talents. And you've helped us by uncovering another portion of this smuggling ring. What we need to stay focused on is the connection between Elodie and the man she met at *Ship's Aground* tavern. Tell us any information she gave you."

"I approached Elodie to see if she'd be interested in working for me as a seamstress."

"That was clever." Amelia noted the surprise in Cord's voice.

"But she works for Helene," Derrick said.

"Yes, but many women have more than one job to support themselves. She knows that I frequently collaborate with Helene and that I also create my own fashion projects. I asked her if she'd like to do extra sewing for me in addition to her work for Helene. She has two younger sisters she supports. I tried very hard to find out where she lived, but she wouldn't tell me. I believe she was trying to protect her father."

"She told you about her father?" Cord asked.

"No, but when I saw the bruises on her arms I knew that she had been mistreated. I assumed it was a man who injured her."

Both men were silent at these revelations.

"From talking with her about her care for her younger sisters, I didn't believe Elodie was the mastermind behind a smuggling ring, but the man who abuses her might be forcing her to play a part."

"This is when you should've told me." Derrick leaned forward, then sat back crossing one of his muscular legs over the other, trying to find a way to fit into the small chair he overfilled.

"But she is young and I wanted to help her. What would happen to her if that man found out that we were on to her?"

Derrick jerked forward as if he wanted to reach across and shake her. "Unbelievable! You're protecting a girl you don't know. But what if the man you're worried about abusing her finds out you're on to *him*. Have you thought about that?"

She shook her head. "You're right. I didn't think my interest in Elodie would raise any suspicions."

Cord ran his hands through his hair. "Elodie's father is our only connection. We must assume he did the stabbing."

"It was my fault he escaped, wasn't it? If I hadn't caused the fight, none of this would've happened."

Cord shook his head. "No, you weren't at fault. Talley had the father and Elodie surrounded. But the father used Elodie, keeping her at knifepoint, to make his escape."

Amelia's stomach plummeted as if she had fallen off a high place. She had never been exposed to such evilness in a parent.

"Talley planned to bring the girl in for questioning. In the ensuing chaos, Elodie fled when her father shoved her into the crowd and made his escape. Talley and his men chased him giving time for Elodie to bolt."

"Oh, that poor girl. Her father is a monster." Amelia dabbed her nose with the twisted handkerchief.

Cord nodded in agreement.

"Have you identified the man he stabbed in the tavern?" Amelia asked.

Cord sat up in his chair. "No. He isn't familiar to us and the Navy didn't recognize him either. He is French and either part of the smuggling ring or part of the criminal element that resides in *Ship's Aground*. We have no way of knowing until we find Elodie's father." His words were clipped and aggressive.

Amelia caught a glimpse of the formidable spy he had been. "But what about Elodie? What will happen to her?"

"We'll follow her from work and find out where she and her father live. Then we'll capture her father and hopefully he'll lead us to who is behind the buying and selling of the Navy's secrets," Cord said. "I don't believe he's a big fish, but we may be able to use him to bring down the entire group."

"You shouldn't punish Elodie. She's a victim. I'm sure her father forced her to do his bidding."

"We're only interested in her father. Unfortunately, right now she's our only tangible lead to her father and the smuggling ring. She might know other of her father's associates."

Amelia worried for the young girl who was in the center of so much danger.

"You realize, when Helene finds out about Elodie's involvement, she'll dismiss her," Cord said.

Amelia felt her stomach clench with helplessness. "Yes, I know that Helene will be forced to fire her. It was what I had hoped to prevent."

Cord leaned forward and patted her hand. "I admire your effort in trying to protect your friend and Elodie. It's very difficult to see an innocent trapped in her parent's criminal activities."

She tried to blink away the burning sensation behind her eyes. Derrick shifted again in his chair.

"And thank you for not including Gwyneth in your visit to the *Ship's Aground*. If anything had happened to her, Ash would've been…" Cord shrugged his shoulders as if shaking off the feelings. "It was awful when Henrietta was almost killed trying to protect her brother."

Amelia felt the first genuine smile of the morning. She respected Cord for his ability to admit to his fears concerning his love for Henrietta. She hoped someday she'd meet a man who could allow himself to express his true feelings. She looked across at Derrick.

His face was compressed in an emotion she couldn't untangle.

Cord stood and walked to the door. He turned back. "Amelia, thank you for your help. We can take it from here."

CHAPTER EIGHTEEN

Brinsley could barely control himself. He was a strange mix of explosive rage and icy fear. Amelia again had pushed him beyond any human's ability to cope. He tried to steady his rapid breathing driven by the dread and anxiety cramping his gut and lungs. He could barely restrain the overwhelming urge to both shake and kiss her senseless.

He didn't want to think about what the men might have done to her last night if he hadn't been present in the tavern. He didn't sleep; reliving all the horrible ways Amelia could possibly have been hurt. The unwanted, disturbing images fueled his anger.

Amelia sat primly across from him, appearing not to have suffered from her adventures. She hadn't realized her jeopardy last night. Of course, she couldn't. She wouldn't look so pleased with herself if she had. The fiery mane that caused a roomful of vicious men to brawl was now tucked into a knot at the back of her neck.

Did she realize the living hell she had put him through when he recognized her? Did she care? All she seemed to consider was the safety of her friends. What about his feelings? His fear? His distress?

She remained seated, apparently in no rush to leave. The gentlemanly thing would be for him to follow Cord's lead of calm and concern, but he had never felt gentlemanly toward Amelia. Lustful, possessive, greedy, yes, but never gentlemanly.

"Why is it that your fiancée didn't accompany you on your

little adventure last night?" He leaned forward, resting his elbows on his knees, trying to look nonchalant when jealousy burned like acid in his gut. "Were you unable to hoodwink him into cooperating in your scatter-brained plan?"

She puffed up in outrage, her pert breasts pushed against her dress. "Of all the nerve." Her face was flushed and she opened her mouth and then closed it again. "My fiancée?"

"Kendal."

She leaned toward him. "I'm not affianced to Michael. Where would you get such a crazy idea?"

He sat up straight. He didn't want to reveal his painful jealousy fueled by watching her intimate dance with Kendal. "Lady Beaumont told me you were to be engaged."

"Aunt Euphemia?" She shook her head in surprise. "Why would she think that?"

Bitterness seized his throat. "By your obvious, intensely intimate dance. The man couldn't take his eyes off your chest. He looked ready to devour you."

Amelia laughed aloud. "Michael has no such feelings toward me."

His hurt and resentment came pouring out. She had laughed at the pain embedded in his brain and heart. "You could've fooled me by the way you danced together."

Amelia stared at him. Her fathomless eyes searched his face.

"Michael and I are childhood friends. Nothing more."

"Ash told me that you wanted to marry Kendal."

Two pink spots bloomed on her cheeks. "Ash didn't know. He was repeating what Gwyneth told him about my childhood fantasies."

He had no desire to hear about her past with Kendal.

He crossed his leg, feigning a nonchalance he didn't possess. "It doesn't matter any longer." As if it didn't matter, when it mattered greatly to him.

Ignoring his sneer, she leaned close enough to touch him. "I did believe I was in love with Michael." Her voice got soft and appealing. "But I was mistaken. I don't love Michael in that way."

"You don't?" He hated that his voice sounded high-pitched and hopeful.

Her lip curved into a coy smile. "I realized that I confused my deep affection for Michael as romantic love. But my feelings for another man clarified the difference."

He should've gotten up and walked away, but her words locked him into the chair; he was trapped. He tried to tell himself that he didn't care, but he did.

Her voice was playful and her eyes danced. "This man has turned my whole world upside down with his demanding kisses and potent stares."

Why was she tormenting him? Didn't she know how much he wanted and needed her?

He stood to leave. There was nothing else to be said.

"And you call yourself a spy?" She had the same teasing tone she had used during the cricket match. She jumped to her feet, facing him toe to toe. "Derrick Jeremy Randolph Brinsley, don't you dare walk out on me. I want you, only you."

"What?" Frozen, he stood there struck dumb like a lummox.

She leaned closer. "Don't act so surprised. You've been trying to seduce me since the minute I met you."

"I…" He couldn't deny the truth.

She now toyed with the buttons on his jacket. "I'm sorry. I have no experience in seducing men, but I want you to do all the things you've been promising with your looks and touches since the first night we kissed."

She leaned closer, pulling on his coat. The blood roared, surging through his body. He could smell the sweet scent of honeysuckle and Amelia. He had to swallow hard before he could speak. He was ready to fulfill her every wish. "You're not in love with Kendal?"

"No. I love him as a friend, with great affection." She looked up at him. Her eyes sparkling and her lips parted…inviting.

She put her hand on his chest. "I don't want Michael like I want you."

He was having trouble catching up with this dramatic change.

He knew she felt the attraction between them, but she wasn't like other women who just wanted him for his bad boy reputation.

It was taking all his self-control to not touch her. Once he touched her, he wouldn't be able to continue this conversation.

"You realized you don't love Kendal, because you lust after me."

Her skin had the pink-tinged flush. Her breathing had changed. She looked into his eyes. "Yes."

"Well, I guess we're in the same situation. Because I've lusted after you since the first time I laid eyes on you." He pulled her into his arms and gave her a searing, possessive kiss. His mouth closed over hers. He wanted her to know that she belonged to him and no one else. "You know what this means, Amelia?" he growled.

She melted against him. The look of total bewilderment on her face did a lot to soothe his male ego and ease the torment she had subjected him to over the last month.

Her eyes were soft and filled with passion. "Amelia?"

"Yes, Derrick." Her voice was breathless and his entire body tightened.

"You know what this means?"

Her creamy skin had a rose-tinged color. And the color heightened on her face. "We're going to be lovers."

"What?" He swallowed against the panic in his throat. He wasn't prepared to declare himself. He was still adjusting to the idea that she wasn't in love with Kendal. "We're going to be lovers once we're married."

She pressed against his erection and moaned, a sweet feminine sound that was moving to a point of no return. Maybe they would be lovers *before* they were married.

His body throbbed with need. She was offering herself. She was an innocent, but she had demonstrated how sensual and responsive she could be. "Why now, after all our time together? Is this some sort of reaction to last night's trauma?"

She pulled out of his arms. "Of course not. I'm totally fine about last night. I wanted to tell you right after my dance with Michael. I hadn't seen Michael since he went to France. And I didn't feel as if I could move forward until I talked with him. Then he was gone on another mission and I had to wait. But I'm glad, since it gave me more time to sort out my feelings."

"But how do I know this isn't an impulsive reaction rather like last night's adventure." He didn't want to think of her as fickle. She didn't seem flighty, but after last night's escapade, he was feeling a bit shaky with this reversal.

She took his hand and pulled him to sit next to her on the settee. Her leg was pressed against him. He could feel the heat of her soft thigh.

"When my mother died, my entire world crumbled. Michael understood when no one else did. My father and brothers were all in shock. And I was jealous that Henrietta still had her mother. I spent a great deal of time with him and my brothers, but he always made a point of taking special care of me when I felt I had no one. He became the center of all my childhood dreams, but I realized I loved him as a friend, a brother. Until I met you, I've never been attracted to anyone else. I've had loads of suitors, but eventually they all became friends or went elsewhere. I'm comfortable with men because of my brothers. Until I met you, I had no idea about burning attraction."

His heart launched into a wild, frantic rhythm. He was still having trouble accepting that Amelia wanted him as much as he wanted her.

"Amelia, I've never met anyone like you, and it isn't just physical attraction. You're kind, devoted to your friends and family. You make me joyful. I haven't felt like that in so long. I admire you, and I want to be part of your life for a long time…for forever."

"Oh, Derrick." Amelia touched his face tenderly. "I hoped you felt the same as I do, but with your reputation, and the way you behaved with Lady Rowley. I didn't know what to think. I didn't think you wanted to settle down."

"I was an ass. Can you forgive me? I was boiling with

jealousy, watching you and Kendal dance together. The way he looked at you. I'd still like to kill him."

"No, he was teasing me about how alluring I'd become as a woman. I think he saw a woman, intent on seducing the man of her dreams."

"Me?" He moved closer to her.

"Yes, Derrick. Only you."

He took her hand into his and stared into her eyes. "And I want you, only you. I've never felt this about anyone until I met you. I want everything with you."

"You do?"

"Will you marry me Amelia?" He pressed her hand to his heart.

"Yes, Derrick. But does this mean we have to wait to be lovers?"

CHAPTER NINETEEN

Amelia couldn't believe the change in Derrick. Once she declared her feelings, he became a marauding, hungry male who couldn't get enough of her. He held her head in his large hands and consumed her mouth. He licked, prodded, sucked. She reveled in his primitive need, kissing him back with the same frantic fervor.

She melted into the overwhelming sensations, floating on a voluptuous wave. Between the love bites and tastes on her neck, he told her that she belonged to him now and he'd never let her go.

Her hot and prickly skin was ultrasensitive to his every touch, as his bristly jaw abraded her throat and his tongue traced her ear.

His harsh, winded breath on her neck and throat excited her, causing her body to melt and her breath to come in short bursts.

She needed to lie with him, to press her entire self against his hard, hot body. "Derrick, please. Let me lie down." she was entirely focused on melding as one with Derrick when he suddenly sat up to disentangle from their passionate embrace.

Amelia heard a loud harrumph and a fake cough before she recognized Gwyneth's voice. "Solving the smuggling ring, I see." And then she broke into peals of laughter. Ash was grinning like a Cheshire cat.

Derrick leapt to his feet and tried to hide Amelia behind him, which made Gwyneth chuckle even more. "A bit late, Brinsley."

Amelia rearranged her hair, which had come undone from its pins and then stood next to him.

"This is becoming a habit for you two," Ash said.

She felt Derrick's body stiffen and knew he wouldn't tolerate much more joking from those two. She stepped around him, but he pulled her to his side. "This is going to become a regular habit as Miss Amelia becomes my wife."

Gwyneth squealed and leapt forward to take Amelia into her arms. "I knew you were in love." Gwyneth didn't let go of Amelia. "Didn't I, Ash?"

Ash rolled his eyes. "It appears you were right."

Ash thumped Derrick on the back."Congratulations on winning the hand of the fearsome Miss Amelia Bonnington."

"We will be brides together, then we can have daughters who will be the closest of friends," Gwyneth gushed.

"Let go of the poor woman, Gwyneth," Ash said. "You don't have to plan her entire future this minute. Besides, I want to offer my solicitations to the bride."

Ash then took Amelia into his arms and hugged her. "I'm so very happy for you, Amelia. And like Gwyneth's sentiments, I consider you both part of our family, sealed after our adventures at the Edworth party." Ash released her to shake Derrick's hand.

Amelia's heart swelled when she saw Derrick's hesitant smile. The poor man looked bewildered, but obviously touched. The man needed family. Whatever happened in his family, Derrick was now obviously alone. She didn't believe for a minute that he had done all those things he was reputed to have done. She knew in her heart, he was honorable.

"I also want to thank you, Amelia, for not involving Gwyneth in last night's caper."

Amelia turned toward Gwyneth. "Can you forgive me for not including you? I'm sorry, but with your demand that Ash not be given a dangerous assignment, I felt it was wrong to include you in the mission before your wedding."

"I'm not mad at you…this time.' Gwyneth's chocolate

brown eyes danced with mischief. "But the next time you dress like a man and venture to a dockside tavern, I want to be involved."

"Gwyneth," Ash's said in a low murmur, but Amelia heard his whisper. "You can dress like a man anytime you want in our boudoir."

Now it was Amelia's turn to laugh as Gwyneth's eyes rounded in interest and her dark skin took on a rosy blush.

Derrick also heard since he chuckled. "Amelia is not engaging in late night adventures any longer." He raised her hand to his lips. "Are you darling?"

How unfair of him to be so tender and attractive. With four charming brothers, she wasn't that easily won over. Her skill at persuading men had been well practiced on her four bullying brothers. "I'm open to negotiating." She looked into his warm eyes, trying to reciprocate the same seductive stare.

He sucked in a long breath.

It was Ash who interrupted their sensual interlude. "I hate to interrupt, but Cord wanted me to discuss the best way to win Madame de Puis' cooperation. Time is of the essence."

Gwyneth took Amelia's arm. "Let's all sit down." She led Amelia to the settee. "You and Brinsley sit here." She then sat in the chair where Cord had been.

Amelia felt the warmth moving to her face as she remembered Derrick and her passion on the settee before they were interrupted. Derrick's muscular thigh pressed against her. He took her hand and caressed it gently between his huge hands. Her heart thumped against her chest. His closeness did strange such strange and delectable things to her.

Ash paced. "I've got a man posted at the front and back of the shop, watching for Elodie. But I wanted to talk with you, Amelia, before I alerted Madame de Puis about the girl."

Amelia tried to pay attention to Ash's words, but Derrick traced her knuckles with his finger. She took a slow breath and tried to focus. "I had an idea while I was speaking with Cord." It was only an hour ago. She stole a peek at Derrick. He was looking down at her with a smoldering stare that turned her insides into jelly.

She needed to help Helene and Elodie. She struggled to ignore her urge to climb into Derrick's lap and kiss him and bite him the way he had done to her.

Ash coughed. "Amelia?"

Gwyneth giggled. "You two are so cute."

That got Amelia. She straightened her spine. "I've been thinking of a way to capture Elodie's father and also to elicit Helene's help."

She ignored Derrick's loud sigh.

"What if I made another doll to look as if it had just arrived...filled with paste diamonds? Wouldn't that push Elodie's father to seek out the traitor? Cord said that you're working off the premise that Elodie's father is an errand boy for one of the French spies."

"That's brilliant. We give him the new diamonds, then he takes them to the French spy, then you watch the French spy make contact with the English traitor." Gwyneth clenched her hands enthusiastically. "Why didn't I think of that?"

Ash smiled in a charming way at his fiancée. "I hope it was because you have had your mind on our wedding." He bent over and whispered, "And our wedding night."

Derrick squeezed Amelia's hand after hearing Ash's erotic promise to Gwyneth.

Ash straightened and looked at Amelia. "How long will it take you to make a doll? We need to find Elodie's father before the next contact."

"With help from two of my maids?"

"I'll help too," Gwyneth said.

Ash beamed at her.

"With the four of us sewing, I can have it done by late afternoon. The shop is open late since ladies need their gowns for tonight's ball."

"What's stopping him from taking the diamonds and making

a run since the French spy doesn't know about this newest doll?" Derrick asked.

"Oh, I didn't think of that." Amelia sat back against the settee.

"But once we see him take the diamonds from the doll, we'll have him in our custody and can convince him to give up his contact," Ash said.

"But how are we going to deliver the doll to Helene?" Gwyneth asked.

"I'll take it to the shop to show Helene. I can pretend my French cousin sent it to me."

Derrick shook his head. "No, you're not going near that shop when…"

Amelia twisted quickly. "But I should be the one to take the doll."

He didn't raise his voice, but said in a quiet dogged way. "I won't risk putting you in danger." He pulled her close. "I can't risk losing you now that I finally have you."

Amelia saw the look of love and worry reflected in his eyes. "I suppose I can send my maid with the doll and a note."

"Helene doesn't need to know anything about the dolls. It will make the whole business easier," Ash said.

CHAPTER TWENTY

Brinsley paced in the subterranean rooms of the Abchurch office. Looking at the two story, brick building, no one would know of the tunnels and cells below the stodgy façade.

He didn't feel the relief and satisfaction after an exemplary completion of the mission. It was too easy. And easy made him uncomfortable. Elodie's father had led them to the English traitor who they captured with the diamonds in-hand. They had thwarted the purchase of the plans for the secret weapon. But something was off, and he had learned from experience to always trust his gut. Something he couldn't pinpoint niggled in the back of his mind.

"Am I boring you?" Ash stood in front of him, giving the details of his interview with the English traitor. "Is your mind on a certain vivacious red-head?"

Brinsley couldn't prevent the wide grin from breaking out across his face, knowing it would spur endless ribbing from Ash. But he was thoroughly taken with the thought of Amelia getting ready for tonight's ball and their first dance—a first step in the initiation of their first lovemaking.

Ash chuckled. "Another rake gets the leg shackle."

Brinsley sat down in a wide wooden chair. Although the atmosphere in the dank basement was gloomy, the chairs in the Abchurch were sturdy, built for a man's comfort. "You're much closer to the shackle than I am."

"Can you blame me?" Ash asked.

"Of course not. You're very fortunate to have won the hand of Lady Gwyneth."

Now it was Ash's turn to smile like a goon. "Did you hear anything I told you?"

"Our traitor was a low-level secretary for the American inventor," Brinsley said.

"Yes. He has no political affiliations I can identify. Looks like he did it for the money."

"Was his contact always Maurice, Elodie's father?" Brinsley asked.

"Yes, but our traitor doesn't think that Maurice was the brains behind the operation. Did Maurice tell you who he stabbed? Could he be the head of the operation?" Ash questioned.

"He said that the French man in the tavern refused to pay for other smuggled goods. Nothing to do with the diamonds."

"A case of bad business between thugs. Do you believe him?"

"I believe him. Maurice is a cutthroat smuggler, not a mastermind. He doesn't have the guts or the ability to run this covert operation. He maintains his instructions came from France and there is no one else involved," Brinsley said.

"He denies having any contacts here?"

"Yes. He spent a great deal of time begging for me to believe that his daughter wasn't involved. That she was totally innocent."

"Do you agree with Amelia, that the young girl is innocent?" Ash asked.

"Yes, but something is bothering me." Brinsley stood.

"I want to follow-up with Madame de Puis. She has to know the French connection who provides Maurice with her fabric and dolls. We should've questioned her sooner."

"We've only known about the diamonds coming through her shop for one day," Ash said. "But I think it's a good idea. I'll finish up with Alfred."

"Alfred?"

"Alfred Pettibone, our Navy secretary, who planned to retire to the Greek islands with the French diamonds. It seems he's always wanted to go abroad."

Brinsley snorted. "The only trip he's going to take is to Newgate." He stood. "I'll see you tonight at the Foster Ball."

Ash clamped his arm around his shoulders. "You better prepare yourself to be the topic of society gossip when you spend the night glued to Amelia's side."

"Amelia doesn't want us to be conspicuous until I've spoken with her father who is out of town. She doesn't want him to hear from anyone else about our engagement."

"Smart girl. Not a good start to get on the bad side of your formidable father-in-law."

"Amelia said the rumors about her father are exaggerated. I believe she used the term pussycat."

Ash laughed out loud. "To his daughter, he might be very sweet, but to the man who is stealing her away, I'd say daunting." Ash's eyes were a bit too bright and his attitude a bit too smug.

"Thanks for your support." Brinsley turned and walked out of the room.

Brinsley wasn't sure if it was all this talk about Amelia and marriage, but he had an urgent need to see and hold her. A disconcerting idea took hold of him while he talked with Ash and he had to act. The most logical contact for the head of the smuggling ring was Helene. She was in the middle of the intrigue. Derrick had no doubt that the French thug had said *elle*—she. He should've suspected Helene sooner.

How did he allow himself to be blinded by Amelia's faith in her friend, to not look at the most likely suspect?

And although Talley had Amelia under surveillance to guard her, he wanted reassurance that she was safe before he went to the modiste's shop.

CHAPTER TWENTY-ONE

Amelia paced between her easel and the west-facing French doors. The afternoon light at the back of Bonnington house was perfect for her painting, and she had spent many creative hours in her studio. Not today. Today she was wound tight. Fear and worry had her nerves coiled into knots. The doll had been sent to the shop several hours earlier. A relaxed Betsy, unaware of her true mission in delivering the doll, stood at the door.

"Miss, you need to get dressed for dinner and the ball."

"Thank you, Betsy. I'll be along in a few minutes. Can you draw a bath for me?" Despite her clammy palms and her heart racing, she maintained the charade of a routine day and not one filled with dangerous spy games.

In the last ten hours, her entire life had been altered. She was now Derrick's fiancée. Her stomach quivered at Derrick's passionate promises during this afternoon's sensual interlude. Derrick vowed to dance with her at the Foster's ball. He wanted to erase all memories of any other man's dance. He wanted her to remember only him and the way he held and looked at her. Her heart fluttered at his possessiveness.

She bent to douse the candles on her desk. She reverently touched the statue of the Etruscan muse, Minerva. Her father had given it to her on her eighteenth birthday. Minerva was the muse of wisdom and art. Her father had always supported her interests, unlike her brothers.

It was time to get ready for the evening. She and Gwyneth, all part of Derrick and Ash's planning to keep them out of harm's way, were to have dinner tonight at Lord Foster's estate before the ball. Lord Foster was an old family friend. After the day's harrowing events, she would've preferred to have the escort of her father and her brothers tonight. But her father had returned to the country for estate business, and Jack and Parker were dining at their clubs.

She heard someone approaching in the hall. Probably Betsy to harangue her to get ready, but it seemed too early for Betsy to return.

"Betsy?" Amelia turned toward the door when it creaked open.

"Elodie?" Amelia stood shocked to see the young girl. Had the plan to follow the seamstress failed?

The young girl bobbed a quick curtsy. "Miss, I'm sorry to bother you, but your butler said I could come back. He recognized me from my other deliveries."

The young girl's hand shook holding the wrapped package.

"Did you bring me fabric?" Amelia's mind spun with the possibilities of what Elodie's appearance could mean.

"No, Miss. I pretended to have fabric. I needed to talk with you. Something terrible…" Elodie's voice broke into a sob. "Some men are following me and I didn't know where to go."

Amelia rushed over to the young girl who remained at the door. Amelia took her arm. "Come and sit down. You're shaking."

"I'm sorry to be a bother, but I don't know what to do."

Amelia guided her to the settee. "You can tell me."

"You've always been so kind." The girl hugged the package to her chest. Tears flowed down her cheeks.

"It's going to be all right." Amelia tried to sound comforting, knowing what awaited Elodie.

Elodie shook her head. "Nothing can be right again."

Amelia sat next to the girl. "I know about your father."

The girl's tear-streaked eyes widened. "You know?"

"That your father makes you take the fashion dolls for him to remove the diamonds."

"I didn't want to do it. Madame has been so good to me. But my father...with his drinking." Her voice trembled. "He wasn't like this when mama was alive. But ever since she died."

"Did you bring the doll I sent to the shop today?" Amelia pointed to the bundle Elodie still held tight against her chest.

Elodie shook her head. "The doll is still at the shop. My father took the diamonds and left."

Amelia squeezed her hand. "What has happened?"

"My father has disappeared. And there are men following me."

"How do you know your father disappeared? He might have stopped off at a tavern."

"He always comes home for luncheon to see to my sisters while I'm at work in the shop. He never forgets the little ones."

This was good news. It must mean that Derrick and Ash had captured him.

Amelia didn't have any reassurances for the girl about her father's future. "Did the men follow you here?"

"No, I'd never lead them to your house, Miss."

"Do you know who these men are?"

"I've never seen them before, but there were two of them. I slipped through into the baker's shop and then went out the back door. I know the back alleys better than anyone."

Amelia didn't know which of Derrick and Ash's subordinates were in charge of watching Elodie, but there would be hell to pay for their blunder.

Amelia patted the girl's hand. "Elodie, you're safe now."

Their strategy appeared to be successful—Derrick had captured Elodie's father and, hopefully, the English traitor selling the Navy's secrets. And Elodie was safe.

Amelia took a deep breath. She didn't realized how tense she had been. Amelia was about to tell the girl that she would help her when the outside French door opened.

"Well, isn't this cozy?" Helene in a dark riding dress with a hood, with her hand on her hip, walked into the studio.

Elodie jumped up. "Madame. Men were following me."

Helene swept her hand in a vicious gesture. "Silence."

"Helene?" Amelia stood. A terrible realization spread through her with revolting speed.

Helene gave a wicked laugh. The harsh hate-thickened sound pierced the silence. "I'm sure you're more than surprised."

The stylish woman flicked her hand and then turned to lock the French doors.

"Elodie, lock the outer door." Helene's voice was awful and ugly.

Elodie stared at her superior, not comprehending her intent, but with a wave of the pistol and a glare, the girl did as she was bid.

"You're the French spy?" Amelia remained incredulous. Her mind was assimilating the obvious facts, but she couldn't grasp them.

Helene lowered her hood. Her dark hair was stylishly wound in coronet braids. She looked the part of any fashionable lady making her afternoon visits, not the mastermind of the French spies, or even the modiste she'd known for years.

"Poor Amelia. You never suspected."

"You're going to laugh, but I was trying to protect you."

"You *are* going to protect me." Helene swept her maroon skirt to the side, as she strode closer.

"You were my friend." Amelia stared at the woman she thought she had known. The betrayal was bitter and bewildering.

For a second the look in Helene's eyes could've been hatred or pity. "Unfortunately, I've no sentiment for friendship. As I've told you, my life is about survival."

"I don't understand," Amelia said.

"You'll be my bargaining chip. I'm sure your good friend Lord Rathbourne will not let his wife's best friend be killed."

Amelia's heart punched against her chest in loud thuds. "You would kill me?"

"Unfortunately, there are always sacrifices when you're fighting a war."

"But why now?"

"Maurice has been captured."

Elodie gasped. "Papa? No." her last word trailed into whimpering sobs.

"And it won't be long before he'll confess. They will tell him they'll imprison his daughters and he'll give me up."

Fear lodged into her throat. Amelia tried to back away, but her legs were against the settee. "If you leave now, you can escape. No one knows you're involved."

"And how long before they'll be searching for me at every port. Your life for my safe passage to France." Helene gave another bitter laugh.

Elodie's sobbing made the tension in the room unbearable. Amelia needed to keep Helene's focus on herself. She didn't trust Helene not to retaliate against Elodie.

"But your work, your shop. Won't you miss it?"

"Miss bowing and groveling to the English? Do you know how tired I am of pretending those British bitches have beauty and taste?"

"You'll return to France after all you suffered there? Or were those stories more of your lies?"

"Napoleon's France has been transformed with the end of the aristocrats. Before Napoleon, we were nothing better than slaves, barely able to eke out a living."

"I realize I never knew you. I thought we shared a love of fashion and art."

"I did like you. You were different. You never treated me as less, but survival gets down to you or me, and I'm not ready to die."

Amelia had never misjudged anyone this badly. Helene was acting as if abducting and killing her friend was normal behavior.

"Time to move. Need to move forward." Helene pulled out a small pistol from beneath her pelisse.

Suddenly Amelia could barely hear above the roaring pulse pounding in her ears. She would die without ever loving

Derrick, without bearing his children. She refused to be intimidated by a madwoman.

"They'll never allow you to escape."

"My dear, you underestimate your influence. Now get over here and start writing a note to Lord Rathbourne."

Terror hit Amelia square in the back of her neck and down her spine. She stood paralyzed.

"Elodie, stop that wailing!" Helene pointed the gun at the young girl. "Sit down and shut up."

Terror-stricken, Elodie sat on the settee. The sound of her gulping, attempting to stifle any sounds, was pitiful.

Amelia walked to her desk. Helene followed her. "You'll direct them that once I'm safely aboard the *Faucon,* they'll find a note at the *Ship's Aground,* instructing them of your whereabouts. Warn them that if they interfere with my passage, they'll never find you alive."

Gross and ugly rage stormed through Amelia. She searched her desk for something to use as a weapon. If she could surprise Helene, she might be able to knock the pistol out of her hand. Surprise was Amelia's only advantage.

Someone pounded on the door. A man's voice—Derrick—shouted, "Amelia!"

Helene turned toward the interruption, giving Amelia the chance to act. She lifted the statue of Minerva and with skills honed on the cricket field, she swung the statue like a bat and hit Helene on the arm, knocking the gun out of her hand as it discharged into the wall. Helene turned on Amelia; rage mottled her face as she grabbed Amelia by the neck.

Amelia, instinctively, brought up her knee for a direct kick to the woman's stomach as she wrestled the woman's hands away from her throat.

Helene gasped in pain and grabbed her abdomen in agony.

Elodie rushed to unlock the door while Amelia fought with Helene. Derrick and Talley, both with pistols drawn, came rushing in.

"Amelia!" Derrick shouted.

Talley grabbed Helene by the arms pulling her away from Amelia, then he leveled his pistol at her.

Stunned by the sudden release, Amelia stared at Derrick, unable to grasp that the crisis was over. He pulled her into his arms. "My God, she had you."

She could feel the terror in his taut body in the way he held her too tight. Amelia's pounding heart matched Derrick's in the same rapid, breathless way. Her knees were still shaky; she was so glad for Derrick's arms.

Derrick didn't let go of Amelia. With open disgust, he spoke to Talley, "Get that vermin out of here. Take her to the Abchurch."

At that moment, two more armed men burst into the room. Talley handed Helene over to one of the muscular men. As they left, Helene kept her back straight and her neck regal as if she were being escorted to the opera or a soirée.

"Keep your gun on her," Talley said to the young man.

Talley pointed with his head toward Elodie. "What about her?"

"You're Elodie Bargeron?" Derrick asked.

Elodie stood, terrified. Her face was grey, her dark eyes wide with terror. She feebly nodded her head.

Turning to Talley, Derrick said, "Take her to Abchurch for questioning."

Amelia tried to pull out of Derrick's arms to reassure Elodie. He resisted and squeezed tighter. "I'm not letting you go."

Amelia looked into his wildly dilated eyes. She realized he needed to hold her as badly as she needed to be surrounded by his strength.

"Elodie, these men will not hurt you. They need to ask you questions about your father."

Tears trickled down the young girl's face. Amelia wanted to comfort her, but Derrick was not about to comply.

"But my sisters, Miss. Who will take care of them?"

"I will have your sisters brought here to my house. And when you're done answering the questions, the men will bring you here to reunite with them. You and your sisters will be safe."

Elodie nodded her head. "Thank you, Miss."

CHAPTER TWENTY-TWO

Brinsley wrapped Amelia in his arms and held her hard against him. He couldn't tell who was shaking more. Her slight body was trembling and cold against him. His heart punched against his chest as if in danger of breaking through.

Despite many treacherous missions, he had never endured danger with a precious loved one. He struggled to gain control of his quaking body and raw feelings.

"I'm glad you arrived when you did," she said against his chest. She tried for a flippant tone, but he could hear the quiver in her voice.

Brinsley shuddered in helpless rage. He tightened his hold, shielding her with his body. He was never going to let her go. The sound of the gunshot echoing behind a locked door before he could break it down would always be seared into his brain. He'd never forget the overpowering helplessness and the accompanying terror. "I was almost too late."

"Your entrance was the perfect distraction I needed to hit the gun out of her hand."

All the muscles in his body bunched rigid and he tried to suck air into his lungs. He couldn't allow himself to think of how close he'd come to losing her. She was inexperienced and had no idea how violently a desperate person might act. He didn't want her ever to experience the evil he had seen. And he didn't want to destroy her confidence that she could have defended herself against a gun-wielding spy. It was his fault that she had been forced into this lethal situation.

His thoughts were getting darker and gloomier with all the possible ways today could've become a deadly disaster.

She snuggled closer to him as if she could read his morbid thoughts. "You're so warm, and I'm so cold."

"You're in shock." He kept her locked to his body, trying to absorb her distress.

"Yes, I do feel a bit wobbly." Her voice and smile were shaky.

He kissed her temple, then her cheek. "Come and sit down."

Holding her close, he led her to the settee. Once there, he carefully set her down, his hands smoothing, touching everywhere. His fingers lightly brushed her neck. "Did she hurt you?"

"No, she didn't want to hurt me. She wanted to use me as a bargaining chip to escape England."

He cursed under his breath. How did he allow himself to be blinded by Amelia's faith in her friend? How had he become so complacent as to accept the intel that the French spy was a man? He should've been more diligent.

Amelia moved closer and ran her hand along his chest. "Derrick, you're blaming yourself, aren't you?"

He looked down at her wan face. With her pale skin and pale lips, the fading bruises on her cheek stood out. She was so damn brave and so incredibly beautiful.

He bent to kiss her, to warm those colorless lips. Suddenly, the door flew open once again and Betsy burst into the room.

"Miss Amelia, are you okay? Stimson told me about Madame de Puis." Betsy's words tumbled out as she rushed toward them. "I can't believe she tried to shoot you." With her curls bobbing around her mobcap, the distressed maid acted as if she were about to throw herself into Amelia's arms.

Derrick wasn't going to allow the entire household to upset Amelia. She had been through hell already without needing to comfort the staff.

Amelia looked up at him and pleaded with those bright eyes for patience. How did she do it? He was known to be a fully competent spy, but Amelia deciphered his intentions easily.

"Betsy, Madame de Puis didn't plan to shoot me. Her gun discharged by accident."

"Oh, Miss." Betsy put her hands to her face. "You could've been shot."

Derrick really didn't want to rehash the horrific experience, and he definitely didn't want Amelia to have to replay her friend's betrayal.

Betsy continued, struggling to regain her composure. "Stimson instructed me to see what your preferences were? Do you want me to summon your brothers? Call the doctor?"

"Thank you, Betsy. I don't believe there is any reason to disturb my brothers."

Amelia looked through her golden eyelashes at Derrick. Did she mean what he thought she did? The idea of them alone together had his body rigid with anticipation.

"Do you want me to fetch the doctor?" Betsy's apple cheeks had turned bright red with all the excitement. The young girl wanted to be of help to her mistress.

"Thank you; I'm fine." Amelia leaned into Derrick's side. Her softness against him sent his heart drumming again, but for a very different reason this time. "But I do need you to find out where Elodie's sisters are. You can ask Stimson to get the information. Take George with you and bring the girls here. Tell Mrs. Wells that we'll have two young girls staying with us, and also Elodie when she returns later tonight."

Betsy nodded. Her youthful face became serious as she listened to her responsibilities. "Is there anything else you'll be needing? Your bath has gone cold. I could fetch tea?"

"No thank you, Betsy. I'm in good hands." Amelia smiled up at Derrick, her tired eyes shining with adoration.

The anger and fear Derrick had held in seemed to melt away and the empty space around his heart became filled instead with an unfamiliar warmth. Her battered face lit up for him. In her distress, she wanted only him.

Betsy gazed innocently, first at Amelia, then at Derrick, then a cheeky smile bloomed on her face.

"That will be all, Betsy," Amelia said.

Betsy bobbed and left.

Finally alone, Derrick pulled Amelia back into his arms, rubbing his hands along her spine. He had to keep touching her. "I was wondering why your brothers hadn't charged in here to rescue you."

"Parker and Jack are out, but they are planning on coming to the Foster Ball to meet you."

He stroked the back of his knuckles along her cheek. "You're not going to a ball after what you just experienced."

She shook her head. Her eyes were clouded with the strain. "I can't go and be with all the people."

"Of course not. You need to rest."

"Derrick, I don't want to be alone." She chewed on her lower lip.

He had no plans to leave her tonight. He needed her too much.

"If I'm alone, I'll think about Helene. And I don't want to think. Not tonight. It's too awful. Too fresh." Now that there were no more distractions, realization of the very real danger she'd been in could settle in. Her voice began to tremble with unshed tears and no longer needed adrenaline.

He ran his hand up and down her arms to sooth her trembling and to reassure himself that she was whole. "Do you want Lady Gwyneth or Lady Henrietta to come and stay with you?"

"Derrick, I want to be with you, only you."

"Honey, it's what I want. I'll take you to your room. I'll get someone to rewarm your bath." He was trying to be noble, but he didn't want to be separated from her.

"Forget the bath; I don't want to be away from you, not even that long. It's going to be hard to not think about..." She swallowed hard. Threatening tears turned her nose red. "She was my friend."

He looked at her ashen face, taking in the way her lower lip quavered.

"Let me stay with you, Amelia. You can take some laudanum and I'll stay with you until you fall asleep."

She pulled out of his arms and tenderly held his face with her palm. "Derrick, I don't need laudanum. I need only you."

She stared up at him, her violet eyes darkened with emotion. "You need me to comfort you, and I need you to comfort me."

His heart swelled against his chest, reacting to her tenderness and love. Did she have any idea what he needed for comfort—a primed male wanting to avenge the woman he loved?

She traced his lips with a delicate finger. He was spellbound, standing immobile as primitive needs filled him. He was wired and ready to explode. She was an innocent. A virgin. And all he could think about was making her his in a very male way.

"I know exactly what you need," she whispered. "I need it too."

"You do?" His voice was husky and rough. Could she mean what he hoped?

"You're so tense and tight, and you're blaming yourself for tonight. You need to relax. And I need to help you."

"Amelia, you're not helping me relax with that sultry look in your eyes. I'm wound up tight." She might be innocent, but she was definitely a determined woman. His woman was no wilting flower.

"You are?" There was a teasing tone in her voice as she pulled out every sensual weapon she knew of.

"Shall I show you?" What he would like to show her, but not tonight. They'd have plenty of nights together. He brushed the corner of her mouth with his thumb. "I'm going to taste you here."

Her bright eyes widened with his touch.

"Then I want to taste you here." He brushed his knuckle over her left nipple.

Her luscious lips opened and her breath came in short pants.

He trailed his hands down her ribs and over her stomach. He stopped. He was going to be out of control if he continued to tell her explicitly how he wanted to taste and devour her.

She swayed toward him. Breathless, she asked, "Can you show me upstairs in my bedroom?"

"Honey, are you sure this is what you want? I'm not sure I can show much restraint tonight after what just happened."

"No restraint?" She pressed her soft curves against him, ratcheting his need. "You promise?" Her eager and mischievous tone was too much for a man barely in control.

His blood surged like hot flames. "I'm showing incredible restraint right now." Hell, he was a bloody saint. "I've wanted you since our first kiss." His fear of losing her, and his basic male need to claim her, coalesced into a burning desire. It had never been like this before.

He sealed his mouth over hers and showed her what he wanted, his tongue plunging in and out of her mouth in unabashed hunger.

She melted against him, her entire body slack in submission. He lifted her into his arms and carried her out the door.

CHAPTER TWENTY-THREE

Amelia cuddled against Derrick's muscular chest as he carried her up the long stairway. She could feel the pounding of his heart—steady and strong.

Derrick had scanned the hallway for Stimson's presence before carrying her up the stairs. After today's calamity, she didn't care if they were seen by the servants, she cared only about being with Derrick.

Her friend's betrayal fell by the wayside. Tonight she wanted Derrick's comfort and love.

The muffled sound of voices could be heard in the distance as they climbed the long, winding staircase. Stimson and the servants were all busy with Talley and his men.

Still in his arms, she opened her bedroom door. Derrick closed the door with a kick, never loosening his hold on her.

The shelter of his arms soothed the strain from the harrowing disaster of the evening. She whispered against his chest, "Lock the door, I don't want anyone to disturb us."

He turned and locked the door then carried her to the flaming fire. He slowly allowed her to slide her down his hard body. The friction caused her body to throb, heating her from the inside out.

He pressed small love bites to her jaw, her chin, her throat. "Are you sure about this?"

She shivered. He kept kissing her, the damp trail left behind along her neck made her tremble with anticipation. She found it hard to stand, her knees unsteady and shaky.

"Are you sure you don't want a bath and sleep?"

She had never known desire could cause such bold recklessness. "I don't want to sleep. I want to live. I've waited too long for you. And nothing is going to stop me. No gun-wielding French spy can change how I feel about you. I love you, Derrick."

His large hands gently framed her face and he kissed her. Not hard and demanding, but tender, slow, and easy.

She wrapped her arms around his neck to pull him closer. He stroked his thumbs over her face as she traced the seams of his lips. When he opened his mouth, she touched her tongue to his.

He groaned loudly and sealed his mouth over hers, hungry and demanding; as if he wanted to devour her. He thrust his tongue in and out, bringing a rosy flush pleasure to her skin. She sucked on his tongue, holding him in her mouth.

Derrick's rough moans in response sent electric thrills through her body.

He stroked down her back to her derriere, exploring and squeezing.

She grasped his shoulders tighter and leaned against him.

Her heart beat harder, faster. She wanted to touch him and excite him as he did her. She wanted him on top of her, pressing his heat into her. Eagerness left her breathless.

"May I play your lady's maid?"

She could barely speak. Her breath came in fits. She nodded.

His desperation to undress her fed her own frantic desire. The surges of his hot breath on her neck and the way his hands shook as he loosened her stays, inflamed her senses. She was ready to combust.

Derrick had her out of her dress and stays faster than Betsy. He turned her so that she stood in front of him in only her chemise.

His eyes smoldering with passion, he ran his finger down her front. His touch, slick on the silk, left a flame of sensations in its wake. "You are beautiful, Amelia Bonnington."

His fervent study of her body exhilarated her. His broad chest heaving, his eyes bright with excitement, made her feel triumphant and exuberant. Derrick Brinsley needing her was a very heady feeling.

"Do you know how long I've fantasized about whether you were red all over?" He asked in a low and husky voice.

Warmth slid down her throat, down her breasts to her stomach and beyond. She was gasping. Did men always talk like this during lovemaking? She couldn't believe how he fuelled the need and tension in her body.

His hungry gaze and his rough, gravelly voice made her weak behind her knees. She wanted… "I want to see you too. A girl does have her own fantasies."

Derrick laughed out loud, his wide chest straining against his waistcoat. "I didn't think proper young ladies had such naughty thoughts."

She moved closer to unbutton his coat. "I could never be a proper lady when I have four brothers who show no discretion in front of their sister. I've heard more jokes about pump handles than any woman should be subjected to. But I did wonder about the size of your pump handle."

He gulped then took a slow, deep breath, his strong throat undulating.

She felt daring and even brave, wanting to please him. She brazenly lowered her hand down the front of his breeches as she watched his face. She loved the hitch in his breath, the way his nostrils flared when her hand rubbed him. "You have an impressive pump handle."

"You're killing me, honey." He gave a short choke of laughter, then swept her up and carried her to the bed. "Amelia, I'd love for you to explore, but I don't think I can last."

He placed her next to the bed and slowly removed her chemise. Chills raced along her skin and made her breasts tighten. Suddenly naked, she felt shy and knew her skin was going to turn an unsightly red, now far more revealed than anyone ever saw.

He took both breasts into his hot hands, massaging,

caressing. She was lost to the sensation and to the expression of wonder on his face. He held each breast tightly, then with his thumbs, he toyed with the tips until they grew taut. He bent and took her right breast in his mouth.

She gasped and her legs threatened to turn to noodles. The roaring pulse in her ears and burning desire shooting through body very nearly carried her utterly away.

He circled the tight bud with his tongue, tugging softly. "You're so lovely. So perfectly formed." His tongue flicked the sensitive nipple. "And here." His wide hand had spread across her stomach as he found her intimate slit.

She couldn't stand any longer. Her knees buckled.

He lifted her onto the bed. Her already sensitive nipples abraded against his rough waistcoat, causing her lower body to throb and clench.

Derrick shed his clothes quickly, revealing his powerfully potent body. Without his clothes, he seemed bigger, more intimidating. His chest was covered with dark hair that trailed down to his bulging erection. He was ready to couple with her.

She opened her arms to him.

He bent over her. "I'll never forget this moment, Amelia. You open and wanting me."

He carefully positioned himself on top of her, keeping his weight on his elbows.

She opened her legs wider, wanting his heat and strength against her. A sweet ache curled inside her with the way his wiry chest hair brushed against her breasts, and his hard length pressed against her mound—they fit together perfectly.

His body shuddered over her. "Amelia, you feel so good." He nudged his erection against her. She became aware only of the feeling of his hardness against her softness. She pushed against him.

"Oh, honey." He was winded, his chest heaving. "Not yet."

He rolled to his side and gathered her next to him. She could feel his heart pounding against her thrashing heart as if they beat as one.

He took her tight nipple into his mouth as he explored her thighs with his rough hand. He teased with his finger into her curls, spreading her intimately.

A vibrating moan escaped his lips. "You're wet and ready."

He used his teeth on her nipple, licking, sucking as his finger slipped into her wetness. He slowly thrust his finger into her as he pulled harder on her breast. She was stunned, gasping with exquisite pleasure.

His finger pressed deeper into her, his thumb moving slowly across the sensitive nub. She squirmed and spread her legs wider, unable to stand the pressure building inside her.

Derrick's thick lashes lowered over his blazing eyes. There was a flush across his cheekbones. "Give into it, honey." His voice thickened.

She closed her eyes and drifted into the waves of sensation. She emitted a ragged scream as the ecstasy overtook her and quivering tremors wracked her body. Stars burst before her eyes as she spiraled out of control. She couldn't stop sobbing, as she gulped for air.

Derrick chuckled, his hot breath wafting across her face. "I knew you'd be a screamer."

He smoothed the hair around her face, kissing her temples, her cheeks, her nose. His look was filled with love. His tender gaze overcame the boneless lethargy trying to steal into her body.

She reached between their bodies to touch him, to bring him the pleasure he had brought her. She wrapped her hand around his thick hardness.

Derrick shuddered, his eyes closed. "Oh, honey. Another time. I promise."

He moved quickly, suddenly looming over her. Panting, he stared into her eyes. "I'm going to be gentle, but I'm afraid it will hurt." He nudged against her, pressing into her entrance. A sharp pain burned through her with his slow, and hard intrusion. She squirmed against the sting and the invasion.

He stopped and waited, soothing her with his mouth and

murmuring words of love, assuring her that he never wanted to hurt her, but he needed her so badly.

She slid her palms down his body and pulled him closer, urging him. "I need you too, Derrick. Now."

He began to thrust cautiously, but he was losing control in his wild need for her. The pleasure of his sounds made her open to him instinctively, diminishing the discomfort.

She began to rock her hips upward against him. His moan of primal pleasure excited her. She bent her knees, trying to take more of him with each thrust.

His body trembled roughly, a low groan before he thrust fast into her. "I love you," he shouted, then he let out a loud moan and collapsed on top of her.

She felt the warmth of seed spilling into her.

She squeezed him tight against her, reveling in his pleasure, his hot sweating body pressing her down into the mattress. She finally knew what it felt like to be fully loved by a man.

CHAPTER TWENTY-FOUR

Standing together, Amelia and Henrietta watched Gwyneth dance with Ash. She had an exuberant smile on her face. Her pale pink gown whispered around her legs as Ash swung her into a turn. With the coral red ribbon under the bodice and the coral red tiara holding her raven curls into a coronet, Gwyneth was as stunning as Amelia had hoped for.

"You outshone yourself with our lovely gowns," Henrietta said as she unconsciously patted her stomach. "I love this yellow gown and the way it hides my growing bump. It's perfect—simple, but elegant. You know exactly how to make each of us look special."

Amelia smiled at her shorter friend. "You look beautiful. Your pregnancy must be agreeing with you. Your skin is no longer gray and you truly are glowing."

Gowns helped a woman feel attractive, but it was deep joy that glowed in both her friends' faces making them radiant. Amelia now understood, because she knew she also had the look of a woman who was deeply loved.

"It's remarkable, but I started feeling miraculously better a few days ago."

"I'm glad. You did have a rough time," Amelia said.

A self-satisfied smile spread across Henrietta's face. "It was awful. I'm very grateful to have finished this phase. But enough of my pregnancy; I'm sure everyone is tired of hearing about my daily difficulties."

"We all care about you and your baby."

Henrietta touched her stomach again. "But to finish our discussion about our gowns—you look ravishing in purple. Of course, you don't call this color anything as mundane as purple."

Amelia smoothed the lustrous silk floating down from her ribbon-decorated bodice. "This color is *zinzolin.* The dye is made from sesame seeds."

"And I called it purple." Henrietta laughed. "I'm hopeless."

"I wanted to wear a red dress tonight. Voila—*zinzolin,* a reddish violet. I had to find a red with enough blue so it wouldn't clash with my red hair."

"The *zinzolin* makes the red in your hair more vibrant and darkens your eyes. You look exotic, especially with transparent sleeves. Quite daring. You'll start a new fashion."

"The translucent silk inspired me to try the sleeves. Do you like them?"

"I do, but you know I'm terrible at fashion. But I thought tonight's dress would have a very low cut décolletage."

"Derrick asked me to save the low cut dresses for him only. He's quite possessive and doesn't want any other man to touch or look at me. I'm sure he'll relax after we're married."

Henrietta snorted. "Men like Derrick and Cord don't get past their possessiveness. And now that I'm pregnant, Cord has become worse. He doesn't want me to do my code work. He wants me to spend all my time resting. You just wait. I believe its part of their personalities—a need for control."

"You're probably right. Derrick reminds me a lot of my brothers and my father." Amelia searched the ballroom for Derrick. He stood on the other side in a group with her brothers, and her father. Watching him in his black formal wear standing next to her behemoth brothers and father, he looked totally gorgeous and quite comfortable in the men's company. The men were all laughing, and Jack punched Derrick in the arm.

"Your father and brothers are like Derrick and Cord—accustomed to dominating other men, and playing the hero to women," Henrietta said.

"Is Cord totally in control of your marriage?"

Henrietta gave a coy smile. "He's in control of the most pleasing parts."

After her passionate night with Derrick, Amelia understood Henrietta's comment. Derrick had been masterly in his loving, and the memory of his skill in bringing both of them to passion was warming her face. She needed to change the subject or soon she'd be the color of a strawberry.

"Have you been able to return to your work? I'm sure they miss your code-breaking talents."

"My morning sickness has made work difficult, but I believe I've caught up with what's on my desk. Your discovery of the smuggling ring made a big difference in stopping the French from stealing secrets. You have talents in the spy business."

"Thank you, but, unlike Gwyneth, I've no desire to be part of undercover intrigue. I'm going back to my art and design."

Henrietta placed her gloved hand on Amelia's arm. "I'm sorry about Helene. I know she was a friend. It must be difficult to be so betrayed."

"I'm getting past my hurt and anger. Cord has been very kind, talking with me about the conflict created by my loyalty to Helene and my inability to see through her cover. He's been very helpful. Thank you, I know you asked him to speak to me."

"You're my closest friend and I knew Cord would be able to make more sense of what it's like to be caught up in intrigue. But what will happen to the shop?"

Amelia's stomach did somersaults and she felt the blush again creeping up her chest and on her cheeks, remembering, after the second time they made love, how Derrick held her tenderly as they spoke of Helene and Elodie's future.

"Derrick is giving me the shop as my wedding present. And I've hired Elodie to run it. I'll consult on designs that interest me, but Elodie will do all the main work."

"How wonderful and how considerate of Derrick." Henrietta squeezed her arm. "But a woman owning her own business. It's unheard of."

"Unheard of, like a woman working as a code breaker?" Amelia and Henrietta laughed together.

"Of course, Derrick would legally own the business." Which made the ladies laugh more.

Henrietta waved. "There's Aunt Euphemia. Oh, lord; what is she wearing tonight?"

"I like Aunt Euphemia's choices."

"You do not." Henrietta's voice was high pitched and incredulous. "You get upset with my choices all the time."

"I like that Aunt Euphemia is comfortable in her own style. She has a very unusual palette for her color choices, but, if you look in nature, some of her choices are no different."

Henrietta looked at Amelia as if she weren't sure if this was a joke or not.

"I'm not joking. Like tonight, she's wearing fuchsia and green. The fuchsia is more like the French color—a brighter, bluish-red. Aunt Euphemia might like those colors since I've seen her wear them many times. I'm not sure if she realizes, but she had matched the colors of her dress to the fuchsia plant. It's part of the reason I like painting nature because there are no restrictions on our color palette as in the world of fashion."

Henrietta giggled behind her fan. "Aunt Euphemia definitely dresses as a full garden then."

Both ladies tittered.

"But who is the beautiful blonde woman and the very brawny man in the kilt with Aunt Euphemia? I don't remember Gwyneth mentioning anyone from Scotland," Amelia said.

Henrietta shook her head. "I know everyone invited since Cord and I are hosting the ball. There is no Scottish relative on Cord's side of the family or none that I know of."

"Aunt Euphemia is headed this way with the couple."

Aunt Euphemia's turban bobbed along. Tonight the turban only sprouted peacock feathers, no nesting birds.

"Henrietta and Amelia, I wanted to introduce you to Laird MacAlister and his lovely wife, Lauren MacAlister."

Amelia and Henrietta curtsied to the attractive woman. "It's a pleasure to meet you," Amelia chimed. Henrietta smiled and nodded.

"Lauren grew up next to Brinsley." Aunt Euphemia looked at Amelia with an expectant look.

Lauren stepped closer to Amelia. "I'm Baron Lyon's daughter. I was the Marquis of Falconridge's fiancée."

Amelia felt like she was in a play, but didn't know the script. There was silence all around them. The music had stopped playing and everyone was listening.

Lauren looked up into her husband's face. He looked down affectionately and gave her arm a squeeze. "I'm the woman Derrick helped to escape from a terrible marriage to his brother. He took me to Scotland."

Shock choked Amelia. She drew a breath, then another.

"And I was fortunate to meet the bonny lass." Laird Mac Alister beamed. His reddish hair was almost the same shade as Amelia's.

Stupefied, Amelia watched Derrick moving quickly toward them, taking long strides across the dance floor. Thank goodness the dancing had stopped. His face was inscrutable, tight with an unknown emotion.

The only sound in the ballroom was the hushed conversations taking place in isolated groups around the room. Everyone was watching, waiting for a spectacle. All eyes tracked Derrick's movement across the floor.

Derrick stepped around Lauren and took Amelia's arm. "Honey, I want you to meet my childhood friend."

Understanding their need for privacy, Henrietta and Aunt Euphemia stood aside and spoke quietly to each other.

Amelia relaxed with the warmth of his arm and greeting.

Lauren curtsied to Derrick. "I had the pleasure of meeting Miss Amelia. I hear that congratulations are in order. But first, I'd like you to meet my husband, Laird Connor MacAlister."

"Husband?" Derrick raised his eyebrows at Lauren then pulled her into his arms. "I'm so happy for you, Lauren."

Connor and Amelia both stared at the couple, unsure of their roles.

"I'd be needing to take Brinsley down if he hadn't saved my lovely Lauren for me," said Connor.

Derrick released Lauren and pounded Connor on the back. "You're a lucky man. Lauren is a very special woman."

Connor obviously wasn't used to such a show of emotion. He nodded. "Thank you for taking care of her. I owe you a great debt."

"There is no debt." Derrick pulled Amelia to his side. "It appears we both have met our perfect partners."

Derrick was overwhelmed with the shock of seeing Lauren, and dismay for Amelia to have to play a part in the public spectacle.

"I'd like to have a few moments with Miss Amelia. I'm sure this comes as much as a surprise to her as to me." Derrick pulled Amelia closer to him. Her face was pink, not the wan pallor when he first joined the group. He hated that he had enmeshed her in his family mess.

Lauren touched Derrick on the arm. "I apologize, Brinsley, if I've caused you any embarrassment, but your Aunt Euphemia was insistent that we make a very public appearance to help quell all the rumors once and for all."

"You needn't apologize, Lauren. I'll always be grateful to you and MacAlister for attending the ball." Derrick could feel his voice tighten with emotion. This development would restore his reputation, but he wished that Amelia didn't have to be part of the old scandal.

Amelia pulled away from him and took Lauren's hands into her own. "Thank you for helping Derrick come back into society." Amelia's eyes teared and her voice quivered.

Derrick couldn't have felt more love for his generous and gracious Amelia. He wasn't sure he deserved her, but he would take good care of his treasure.

Lauren shook her head as Amelia stepped back. "It appears you already brought him back. And I'm glad; no one deserves love and happiness more than Brinsley."

Derrick felt his face flare with heat. He couldn't endure more of this public discussion.

Amelia took his arm, showing her understanding of his embarrassment. "Will you join us for tea tomorrow? Derrick will be braving teatime, or maybe more accurately pandemonium time, with my four brothers and my father. We'd love to have you join us," Amelia looked up at him for agreement.

"We wouldn't be intruding?" Connor asked.

Derrick hadn't noticed Aunt Euphemia until she spoke from behind him. She must have been listening to the entire exchange as she stepped forward, the feathers on her turban waving. "I'd like to be included in the invitation."

"Of course, Aunt Euphemia." Amelia nodded with a wide smile. "My father and I would be honored to have you join us."

Derrick stared at the older woman. Her eyes twinkling with tender mischievousness. And if he hadn't been watching closely, he'd have missed her brief wink.

Lauren and Connor exchanged a knowing look. "We'd love to join you."

Amelia's face broke into a wide grin. "Wonderful. I think Derrick would appreciate the support of old friends as he faces my family."

"Tomorrow it is." Derrick said. "And now that we've given the ton enough to talk about for at least six months, I'd like to take my perfect partner for a stroll." Derrick bowed to Aunt Euphemia. And with Amelia on his arm, he turned to the French doors leading onto the balcony. He hoped to escape for a few moments with Amelia. With the appearance of Lauren, every eye was upon them.

He looked down at Amelia, her cheeks flushed from all the attention.

"Would you rather not be with me and not attract further notice until this latest gossip settles down?"

"What? And miss walking next to a hero." Amelia looked up at him with adoring light in her eyes, a small smile curling her lips. "Except, you're my hero now."

"I'm no hero." Derrick shook his head as he opened the door to the outside.

"Tell that to Lauren or to Laird MacAlister. They say you saved her from your brother and a disastrous marriage."

After keeping the secret of the abuse for so long, he still felt the disgrace of his family. He didn't want Amelia to associate him with the iniquity of his family.

She stopped, pulling on his arm to make him pause and look at her. "Derrick, you know I'll never judge you by your family. I would hate to think what people would think if they judged me by my brothers." She laughed, her eyes playful and caring.

He took a deep breath and tried to sound unaffected. "My brother was raised to succeed my father. He learned from my father that a duke must rule by any means, including physical intimidation and cruelty." The old anger started to erupt, but Amelia's loving and accepting look eased the lonely burden.

"You and your mother were the recipients of this cruelty?" She touched him gently on his arm.

The shame and pain burned in his gut. "Aunt Euphemia told you about my mother?"

"No. I overheard Aunt Euphemia mention better times, so I did wonder."

"Aunt Euphemia knew my mother before she married my father. She knows what my mother endured."

Amelia squeezed his arm. "Derrick, I'm sorry."

"You don't have to be sorry. It's over. The old tyrant is gone. I never see my brother."

"Never?" Her brows beetled together.

"I inherited my estate from my mother. Rather poetic justice. My father married my mother for the very profitable estate. Fortunately, my brother didn't benefit from my mother's suffering."

He was so intent on finally sharing the strain of his family's vileness, he didn't notice the other guests moving closer to them.

Rathbourne, with Lady Henrietta on his arm, and Ash, with Lady Gwyneth on his arm, encircled Derrick.

Rathbourne clapped him on his back. "Glad to see you finally vindicated."

"You knew?" Derrick's incredulous face and voice made everyone laugh.

"Of course, I do have access to certain information." Rathbourne said in his usual cool voice.

Lady Gwyneth shook her head at her brother. "I didn't know that Miss Lauren married a Scottish laird, but I always knew, Brinsley, that you were an honorable man."

"An amazing gesture, that Brinsley took Miss Lauren out of his brother's reach," Ash said.

As the ladies all scrutinized Derrick, he couldn't keep his face from heating again.

"Did you know, Amelia?" Gwyneth asked.

"Not until tonight. But like you, Gwyneth, I believed in Derrick."

The ladies sighed and the men, including Derrick, all shifted their weight.

"I believe I hear the instruments warming up for the next dance. Does my bride want to dance again?" Ash teased.

"Of course, I wouldn't miss it." Lady Gwyneth cooed.

"Henrietta?" Rathbourne asked.

"I'd be honored, sir." Henrietta curtsied.

Ash and Rathbourne led the ladies into the ballroom.

"I believe you owe me a dance." Amelia licked her lower lip.

"I believe I owe you a lifetime of dances." And he swept Amelia into his arms.

EPILOGUE

Amelia added extra cream and sugar into Aunt Euphemia's teacup as usual. Aunt Euphemia, dressed in a robin's egg blue afternoon gown with a lime green velvet toque perched on her silver-white hair, looked the part of the respectable matron.

Amelia's younger brothers sat beside her on the settee. She could supervise them better when she kept them in close proximity. Aunt Euphemia sat in one of the many winged chairs arranged around the table. She expected ten for the afternoon's tea.

Aunt Euphemia looked at Drew, the youngest brother, who had stuffed an entire sandwich in his mouth. "Young man, are you a cricket player?"

Colin, older than Drew by one year, replied around the partially-chewed apple slice in his mouth. "He tries."

If their appetites were a predictor, her younger brothers would grow tall and hefty as her older brothers.

Although Aunt Euphemia's toque was secured with ribbons under her chin, the nest of chickadee-like birds perched on the hat veered each time she spoke. "Colin, may I hazard a guess that you're close to fourteen years old."

"Yes, ma'am. I just turned fourteen. Drew is the baby."

"I'm not a baby," Drew screeched.

Amelia shot a stern look at Colin with no effect.

Aunt Euphemia, made of sterner stuff than tea with young hooligans, smiled at both boys. "I'm assuming Jack is next in line to your father."

Drew piped in. "Jack is the oldest, then Amelia, Parker, Colin, and then me."

Colin leaned around Amelia toward Drew. "Don't forget Matilda and Mirabelle. They come before you too."

Amelia issued a gentle warning. "Colin…"

Aunt Euphemia's birds fluttered as her head bobbed. "Matilda and Mirabelle?" She teased. "You have more sisters?"

Drew squealed in delight at the idea of their two dogs as sisters.

Colin rolled his eyes. "One sister is enough."

Amelia sipped her tea. She was used to playing the role of ogre with her brothers.

"Don't keep me in suspense, Colin. Who are Matilda and Mirabelle?" Aunt Euphemia asked innocently.

Asleep by the hearth, the two spaniels, responding to their names, jumped up, and raced to the table.

Drew broke into a fit of giggles. "This is Matilda and this is Mirabelle." He fed each of them a sandwich from the tray, breaking all the rules that Amelia had been trying to drum into their heads.

"Drew, you're not to feed the dogs during tea-time," Amelia said.

Aunt Euphemia chuckled and looked across the room. "I now have met your entire family."

Amelia followed her gaze. Derrick, her father, Parker, and Jack, stood by the large window framing the winter garden of Bonnington estate. Although Derrick's head was tilted, likely listening to a discussion of the newest reform in Parliament, Amelia could feel his heated gaze. She was shocked by his ability to arouse her with only an ardent stare. Was he remembering their passionate night together as she was?

Derrick, noting her stare, spoke briefly to her father before walking toward her. Her heart slammed against her chest in an erratic rhythm.

She couldn't look away, entranced by his passionate and possessive look. His purposeful stride was less like a gentleman, dressed in buff pantaloons and polished Hessians, but rather a marauding pirate ready to abduct her.

And she'd be a willing captive, allowing herself to be swept into his arms and ravaged.

"Amelia, why is your face turning red?" Drew said in a loud voice.

Aunt Euphemia harrumphed behind her napkin.

Amelia stood. "It's warm in here." She stepped around her brother to get to Derrick.

Derrick took her hands into his, pulling her closer to the door, away from peering eyes and listening ears. "You beckoned me?"

"I did?" She looked up into his fervent, penetrating stare.

"You were inviting me to come over and carry you out of this room and away from your family."

"I might have," she whispered. "I was remembering our night together and wanting another."

"My God, Amelia. Don't say anymore or I will embarrass myself."

"You will." She looked down at his pantaloons.

"Don't look, it will only make it worse," Derrick growled. "We have to make this a very short engagement."

Amelia wanted to put her hand under his shirt, to feel his warmth and untie his pristine cravat to reveal his strong throat, but she reminded herself that her entire family was watching. "I don't know myself. All I think about is you and our night."

"Darling, it's the same for me." His voice was warm and gravelly.

And as she leaned toward Derrick, wanting to be as close as socially permissible, Stimson opened the door to announce the arrival of their guests.

Laird MacAlister, with Lauren on one arm and another beautiful young blond woman on the other, entered the drawing room.

Amelia, with her arm laced with Derrick, greeted their guests together.

"Welcome to Bonnington home." Amelia curtsied to Lauren and the young woman who appeared to be Lauren's sister. She had the same round face, slim figure, and rosy cheeks.

Derrick bowed to Lauren. "Lauren. And can this be little Abbie?"

Abbie, pretending to be coquettish, batted her eyes at Derrick. "Yes, Lord Brinsley. It is I, Abbie, all grown.

The young woman, had the same blond curls as Lauren, but, instead of dark eyes, hers were a bright blue. And she had the same mischievous spark as Gwyneth.

Derrick nodded to the Laird. "MacAlister."

Lauren stepped closer to Amelia. "Miss Amelia, may I introduce you to my sister, Miss Abigail."

Parker moved quickly across the room and spoke to Derrick in a low, fascinated voice that Amelia had never previously heard. "I'd like to meet the grown Abbie."

Amelia watched her middle brother turn on his charm for the pleasing and spunky Miss Abigail, who didn't seem impressed by the attention, as if she were accustomed to the intense attention of gentlemen.

With Miss Abigail's disinterest, Parker bowed and moved to the trays filled with food.

Her father and Jack then joined the group for introductions. Jack, in his role as the oldest son, was confident of his ability to charm both ladies.

"Miss Abigail, you're visiting from Scotland?" Jack smiled down at the young woman, assured of his appeal.

"I reside in London, sir. Lauren lives in Scotland." Miss Abigail didn't seem the least impressed by the attention of Amelia's handsomely roguish brother, answering politely.

Jack, who was used to women fawning over him, was in shock. He never had to make an effort with women. With his strong build, good looks, and his irresistible magnetism, he was always in demand by the ladies.

Amelia couldn't believe her brother's expression. His wide eyes and his slack mouth appeared as if he had been struck dumb by Miss Abigail's winsome looks. All he did was stare at the young woman—two spots colored his cheeks.

"London keeps you busy attending balls? Taking in the season?" Jack asked.

"No, sir. I'm not in the least interested in frivolous activities."

"Frivolous activities? How else does a young lady spend her time?"

As is Jack's questions were rhetorical and easily ignored, Miss Abigail put her hand on Amelia's arm. "Lady Beaumont has told me about your talent as an artist, Miss Amelia. I want to hear all about your work."

"Her work?" Jack asked incredulously.

"Yes, work. Do you not believe woman can have meaningful work?" Miss Abigail smiled, displaying a dimple in her cheek.

Derrick whispered into Amelia's ear. "Poor man. He doesn't know what he's in for."

Amelia leaned against Derrick's side. "What is poor Jack facing?"

Derrick laced his fingers through hers. "A lifetime of love and happiness."

THE
CODE BREAKERS
SERIES

A Christmas Code

"SPIES, INTRIGUE, AND A
SUPER SMART HEROINE.
EXACTLY MY TYPE OF REGENCY."
—ROSEMARY JONES, AUTHOR OF
COLD STEEL & SPIES

JACKI DELECKI

AWARD-WINNING AUTHOR

Enjoy an excerpt from

A CHRISTMAS CODE

A Regency Novella, Second in The Code Breaker Series.

Hot and breathless from performing the newly imported French dance steps of the quadrille, Lady Gwyneth paused during the break in the music. She fanned her heated cheeks repeatedly, attempting to cool herself. Lord Henley glanced down at her. His lips were tight, his eyes dark with need. She had seen the same look on the faces of many men, but never on the face of the only man who mattered.

She wanted to see the same burning desire and possessiveness in the eyes of her childhood infatuation as she knew blazed in her eyes when she looked at the impossible but dazzling Viscount Ashworth.

The gentleman, newly arrived, had barely glanced at her despite the new gown made especially to entice the hard-headed rake. Her friend and dress designer, Amelia, obsessed with the simplicity of Greek togas, had crisscrossed sky blue silk across Gwyneth's ample chest with a dramatic décolletage. The back of the gown was draped in the same manner with a revealing V. It was a simple design, but sensual in the way the fabric clung to her body.

She felt alluring and hopeful that tonight Ash would finally throw off all the restraints. She had felt his eyes on her back, knowing he watched her as she gaily danced the intricate pattern she had recently learned from her French dance master.

Lord Henley offered his arm as the quadrille ended. "May I take you to the refreshment table for a glass of punch? This new French dance is very demanding."

"Thank you. I'm not thirsty. Can you please take me to my dear friend, Miss Bonnington?"

Lord Henley's eyes clouded with emotion. Gwyneth couldn't

refuse the dance, but she needed to escape the gentleman before he embarrassed himself. She wanted to spare him the pain of rejection. After five marriage proposals this season, she had become somewhat of an expert in recognizing the signs of imminent declaration.

Lord Henley escorted Gwyneth to Amelia, who had also finished dancing and now stood alone.

"Thank you, sir, for the dance." Gwyneth did a brief curtsy.

Lord Henley bowed. "It was my pleasure." He hesitated, then sharply nodded his head. She didn't want to be unkind, but there was no reason to pretend interest and encourage hope when there was none.

They watched Lord Henley circle to the other side of the room.

Amelia hid her face behind her fan, her bright eyes dancing in merriment. "Another stricken gentleman."

"I believe he was about to ask if he could call on my brother tomorrow. I think I did an excellent job of extricating myself before Lord Henley declared his feelings."

"Lord Henley is quite a catch. He's heir to a vast fortune. His interest can't be limited only to your dowry."

"Thank you. I'm glad it isn't only money that makes me attractive." Gwyneth liked to believe it was her wit, her sparkling eyes, but she knew her position as sister to an earl and heiress to a hefty inheritance gave her a definite cache with the gentleman. And it was just like Amelia to tease her.

"Your following of swains has nothing to do with your luscious figure, your dramatic looks, or your amiable personality. My unique skill as a designer has brought all these gentleman to swoon at your feet." Amelia snickered, which made Gwyneth laugh.

Tears were running down Gwyneth's cheeks. "You do know how to level a woman's confidence."

The comment drove both to louder laughter.

Gwyneth noticed that Ash had turned in her direction. He smiled.

Lost in the merriment, she smiled back before she remembered her resolution not to appear as a puppy, waiting at his feet for a pat on the head. She could hide her feelings as well as he did. Forbidden by some unwritten gentleman's code, Ash considered her off limits. She wasn't sure if it was the age difference of eight years, his rakish past, or her position as his best friend's younger sister.

He still kept her at a distance, maintaining that she was a mere youngster and they were simply childhood friends. She had spent the entire season trying to convince him otherwise, but she was tiring of the game.

Look for more heart-pounding adventure, spies and espionage, and enthralling romance in *A Cantata of Love*, to be released in May, 2015.

ABOUT THE AUTHOR

Jacki Delecki is a Best-Selling, Romantic Suspense writer. Delecki's **Grayce Walters Series**, which chronicles the adventures of a Seattle pet acupuncturist, was an editor's selection by USA Today. Delecki's Romantic Regency **The Code Breaker Series** hit number one on Amazon. Both acclaimed series are available for purchase at www.JackiDelecki.com.

To learn more about Jacki and her books and to be the first to hear about giveaways join her newsletter found on her website: http://www.jackidelecki.com. Follow her on FB—Jacki Delecki; Twitter @jackidelecki.

Made in the USA
San Bernardino, CA
17 December 2016